MY ENEMY'S ENEMY

Also by Kingsley Amis

MY ENEMY'S ENEMY

KINGSLEY AMIS

My enemy's enemy is my friend
—Hebrew Proverb

Harcourt, Brace & World, Inc.
New York

first American edition 1963

Library of Congress Catalog Card Number: 63-11907

Printed in the United States of America

To
MAGGIE AND JONNIE
AERON-THOMAS

ACKNOWLEDGMENTS

My Enemy's Enemy appeared in *Encounter*, 1955, and in *Winter's Tales I*, Macmillan & Co., 1955

Court of Inquiry appeared in the *Spectator*, 1956

Moral Fibre appeared in *Esquire* Magazine, March 1959

Interesting Things appeared in *Pick of Today's Short Stories 7*, Putnam & Co., 1956

All the Blood Within Me appeared in the *Spectator*, 1962

Something Strange appeared in the *Spectator*, 1960, in *Pick of Today's Short Stories 12*, Putnam & Co., 1961, and in *The Magazine of Fantasy and Science Fiction*, 1961

CONTENTS

MY ENEMY'S ENEMY

MY ENEMY'S ENEMY

I

"Yes, I know all about that, Tom," the Adjutant said through a mouthful of stew. "But technical qualifications aren't everything. There's other sides to a Signals officer's job, you know, especially while we're still pretty well static. The communications are running themselves and we don't want to start getting complacent. My personal view is and has been from the word go that your friend Dally's a standing bloody reproach to this unit, never mind how much he knows about the six-channel and the other boxes of tricks. That's a lineman-mechanic's job, anyway, not an officer's. And I can tell you for a fact I mean to do something about it, do you see?" He laid down his knife, though not his fork, and took three or four swallows of wine.

"Well, your boy Cleaver doesn't impress me all that much, Bill," Thurston, who hated the Adjutant, said to him. "The only time we've tried him on duty he flapped."

"Just inexperience, Tom," the Adjutant said. "He'd soon snap out of that if we gave him command of the section. Sergeant Beech would carry him until he found his feet."

"Mm, I'd like to see that, I must say. The line duty-officer getting his sergeant out of bed to hold his hand while he changes a valve."

"Now look here, old boy." The Adjutant levered a piece of meat out from between two teeth and ate it. "You know as well as I do that young Cleaver's got the best technical qualifications of anyone in the whole unit. It's not his fault he's been stuck on office work ever since he came to us. There's a fellow that'd smarten up that bunch of goons and long-haired bloody mathematical wizards they call a line-maintenance section. As it is, the N.C.O.s don't chase the blokes and Dally isn't interested in chasing the N.C.O.s. Isn't interested in anything but his bloody circuit diagrams and test-frames and what-have-you."

To cover his irritation, Thurston summoned the Mess corporal, who stood by the wall in a posture that compromised between that of an attendant waiter and the regulation stand-at-ease position. The Adjutant had schooled him in Mess procedure, though not in Mess etiquette. "Gin and lime, please, Gordon.... Just as well in a way he is interested in line apparatus, isn't it, Bill? We'd have looked pretty silly without him during the move out of Normandy and across France. He worked as hard as any two of the rest of us. And as well."

"He got his bouquet from the Colonel, didn't he? I don't grudge him that, I admit he did good work then. Not as good as some of his chaps, probably, but still, he served his turn. Yes, that's exactly it, Tom, he's served his——"

"According to Major Rylands he was the linchpin of the whole issue," Thurston said, lighting a cigarette with fingers that were starting to tremble. "And I'm prepared to take his word for it. The war isn't over yet, you know. Christ knows what may happen in the spring. If Dally isn't around to hold the line-maintenance end up for Rylands, the whole unit might end up in the muck with the Staff jumping on its back. Cleaver might be all right, I agree. We just can't afford to take the risk."

This was an unusually long speech for anyone below the rank of major to make in the Adjutant's presence. Temporarily gagged by a mouthful of stew, that officer was eating as fast as he could and shaking his forefinger to indicate that he would as soon as possible propose some decisive amendment to what he had just been told. With his other hand he scratched the crown of his glossy black head, looking momentarily like a tick-tack man working through his lunch-break. He said indistinctly: "You're on to the crux of the whole thing, old boy. Rylands is the root of all the trouble. Bad example at the top, do you see?" Swallowing, he went on: "If the second-in-command goes round looking like a latrine detail and calling the blokes by their Christian names, what can you expect? You can't get away from it, familiarity breeds contempt. Trouble with him is he thinks he's still working in the Post Office."

A hot foam of anger seemed to fizz up in Thurston's chest. "Major Rylands is the only field officer in this entire unit who knows his job. It is due to him and Dally, plus Sergeant Beech and the lineman-mechs., that our line communications have worked so smoothly during this campaign. To them and to no one else. If they can go on doing that they can walk about with bare arses for all I care."

The Adjutant frowned at Thurston. After running his tongue round his upper teeth, he said: "You seem to forget, Tom, that I'm responsible for the discipline of officers in this unit." He paused to let the other reflect on the personal implications of this, then nodded to where Corporal Gordon was approaching with Thurston's drink.

As he signed the chit, Thurston was thinking that Gordon had probably been listening to the conversation from the passage. If so, he would probably discuss it with Hill, the Colonel's batman, who would probably report it to his master. It was often said, especially by Lieutenant Dalessio, the "Dally" now under discussion, that the Colonel's chief contact with his unit was through the rumours and allegations Hill and, to a less extent, the Adjutant took to him. A tweak of disquiet made Thurston drink deeply and resolve to say no more for a bit.

The Adjutant was brushing crumbs off his battledress, which was of the greenish hue current in the Canadian Army. This little affectation, like the gamboge gloves and the bamboo walking-stick, perhaps suited a man who had helped to advertise men's clothes in civilian life. He went on to say in his rapid quacking monotone: "I'd advise you, Tom, not to stick your neck out too far in supporting a man who's going to be out of this unit on his ear before very long."

"Rylands, you mean?"

"No no no. Unfortunately not. But Dally's going."

"That's gen, is it?"

"Not yet, but it will be."

"I don't follow you."

The Adjutant looked up in Gordon's direction, then leaned forward across the table to Thurston. "It only needs one more thing," he said quietly, "to turn the scale. The C.O.'s been watching Dally for some time, on my suggestion. I know the old man pretty well, as you know, after being in his Company for three years at North Midland Command. He's waiting to make up his mind, do you see? If Dally puts up a black in the near future—a real black—that'll be enough for the C.O. Cleaver'll get his chance at last."

"Suppose Dally doesn't put up a black?"

"He will."

"He hasn't yet, you know. The terminal equipment's all on the top line, and Dally knows it inside out."

"I'm not talking about that kind of a black. I'm talking about the administrative and disciplinary side. Those vehicles of his are in a shocking condition. I thought of working a snap 406 inspection on one of them, but that wouldn't look too good. Too much like discrimination. But there'll be something. Just give me time."

Thurston thought of saying that those vehicles, though covered with months-old mud and otherwise offensive to the inspecting eye, were in good running order, thanks to the efficiency of the section's transport corporal. Instead, he let his mind wander back to one of the many stories of the Colonel's spell as a company commander in England. Three weeks running he had presented his weekly prize of £1 for the smartest vehicle to the driver of an obsolete wireless-truck immobilised for lack of spare parts. The Company Sergeant-Major had won a bet about it.

"We'll have some fun then, Tom old boy," the Adjutant was saying in as festive a tone as his voice allowed. He was unaware that Thurston disliked him. His own feelings towards Thurston were a mixture of respect and patronage: respect for Thurston's Oxford degree and accent, job at a minor public school, and efficiency as a non-technical officer; patronage for his practice of reading literary magazines and for his vaguely scholarly manner and appearance. The affinity between Thurston's unmilitary look and the more frankly ragamuffin demeanour of Dalessio could hardly explain, the Adjutant wonderingly felt, the otherwise unaccountable tendency of the one to defend the other. It was true that they'd known each other at the officers' training unit at Catterick, but what could that have to do with it? The Adjutant was unaccustomed to having his opinions contested and he now voiced the slight bafflement that had been growing on him for the last few minutes. "It rather beats me," he said, "why you're taking this line about friend Dally. You're not at all thick with him. In fact he seems to needle you whenever he speaks to you. My impression is, old boy, for what it's worth, you've got no bloody use for him at all. And yet you stick up for him. Why?"

Thurston amazed him by saying coldly : "I don't see why the fact that a man's an Italian should be held against him when he does his job as well as anyone in the sodding Army."

"Just a minute, Tom," the Adjutant said, taking a cigarette from his silver case, given him by his mistress in Brussels. "That's being a bit unfair, you know. You ever heard me say a word about Dalessio being an Eyeteye? Never. You were the one who brought it up. It makes no difference to me if a fellow's father's been interned, provided——"

"Uncle."

"All right, uncle, then. As I say, that's no affair of mine. Presumably he's okay from that point of view or he'd never have got here. And that's all there is to it as far as I'm concerned. I'm not holding it against him, not for a moment. I don't quite know where you picked up that impression, old boy."

Thurston shook his head, blushing slightly. "Sorry, Bill," he said. "I must have got it mixed. It used to get on my wick at Catterick, the way some of the blokes took it out of him about his pal Musso and so on. I suppose it must be through that somehow, in a way, I keep feeling people have got it in for him on that score. Sorry." He was not sorry. He knew quite certainly that his charge was well-founded, and that the other's silence about Dalessio's descent was a matter of circumspection. only. If anyone in the Mess admired Mussolini, Thurston suspected, it was the Adjutant, although he kept quiet about that as well. It was tempting to dig at his prejudices on these and other questions, but Thurston did his best never to succumb to that temptation. The Adjutant's displeasure was always strongly urged and sometimes, rumour said, followed up by retaliatory persecution. Enough, dangerously much, had already been said in Dalessio's defence.

The Adjutant's manner had grown genial again and, with a muttered apology, he now offered Thurston a cigarette. "What about another of those?" he asked, pointing his head at Thurston's glass.

"Thank you, I will, but I must be off in a minute. We're opening that teleprinter to the Poles at twenty-hundred and I want to see it's working."

Two more officers now entered the Mess dining-room. They were Captain Bentham, a forty-year-old Regular soldier who had been a company sergeant-major in India at the outbreak of war, and Captain Rowney, who besides being in charge of the unit's administration was also the Mess's catering officer. Rowney nodded to Thurston and

grinned at the Adjutant, whose Canadian battledress he
had been responsible for securing. He himself was wearing
a sheepskin jacket, made on the Belgian black market.
"Hallo William," he said. "Won the war yet?" Although he
was a great chum of the Adjutant's, some of his remarks
to him, Thurston had noticed, carried a curious vein of
satire. Bentham sat stolidly down a couple of places along
the table, running his hands over his thin grey hair.

"Tom and I have been doing a little plotting," the
Adjutant said. "We've decided a certain officer's career with
this unit needs terminating."

Bentham glanced up casually and caught Thurston's
eye. This, coming on top of the Adjutant's misrepresenta-
tion of the recent discussion, made Thurston feel slightly
uncomfortable. That was ludicrous, because he had long
ago written Bentham off as of no particular account, as the
most uninteresting type of Regular Army ex-ranker, good
only at cable-laying, supervising cable-laying and looking
after the men who did the actual cable-laying. Despite this,
Thurston found himself saying : "It wasn't quite like that,"
but at that moment Rowney asked the Adjutant a question
and the protest, mild as it was, went unheard.

"Your friend Dally, of course," the Adjutant answered
Rowney.

"Why, what's he been up to?" Bentham asked in his slow
Yorkshire voice. "Having his hair cut?"

There was a general laugh, then a token silence while
Gordon laid plates of stew in front of the new arrivals. His
inquiry whether the Adjutant wanted any rice pudding was
met with a facetious and impracticable instruction for the
disposal of that foodstuff by an often-quoted route. "Can't
you do better than that, Jack?" the Adjutant asked

Rowney. "Third night we've had Chinese wedding-cake this week."

"Sorry, William. My Belgian friend's had a little mis-understanding with the civvy police. I'm still looking round for another pal with the right views on how the officers of a liberating army should be fed. Just possess your soul in patience."

"What's this about Dally?" Bentham persisted. "If there's a move to give him a wash and a change of clothes, count me in."

Thurston got up before the topic could be reopened. "By the way, Jack," he said to Rowney, "young Malone asked me to remind you that he still hasn't had those cigarettes for the blokes he's lent to Special Wireless."

Rowney sighed. "Tell him it's not my pigeon, will you, Thomas? I've been into it all with him. They're under Special Wireless for everything now."

"Not N.A.A.F.I. rations. He told me you'd agreed to supply them."

"Up until last week. They're off my hands now."

"Oh no they're not," Thurston said nastily. "According to Malone they still haven't had last week's."

"Well, tell him . . ."

"Look, Jack, you tell him. It's nothing to do with me, is it?"

Rowney stared at him. "All right, Thomas," he said, abruptly diving his fork into his stew. "I'll tell him."

Dodging the hanging lamp-shade, which at its lowest point was no more than five feet from the floor, Thurston hurried out, his greatcoat over his arm.

"What's eating our intellectual friend?" Rowney asked.

The Adjutant rubbed his blue chin. "Don't know quite.

He was behaving rather oddly before you blokes came in. He's getting too sort of wrapped up in himself. Needs shaking up." He was just deciding, having previously decided against it, to inflict some small but salutary injustice on Thurston through the medium of unit orders. He might compel the various sections to start handing in their various stores records for check, beginning with Thurston's section and stopping after it. Nice, but perhaps a bit too drastic. What about pinching his jeep for some tiresome extra duty? That might be just the thing.

"If you ask me," Bentham was saying, "he's too bloody stuck-up by half. Wants a lesson of some kind, he does."

"You're going too far there, Ben," the Adjutant said decisively. He disliked having Bentham in the Officers' Mess, declaring its tone to be thereby lowered, and often said he thought the old boy would be much happier back in the Sergeants' Mess with people of his own type. "Tom Thurston's about the only chap round here you can carry on a reasonably intelligent discussion with."

Bentham, unabashed, broke off a piece of bread and ran it round his plate in a way that Thurston and the Adjutant were, unknown to each other, united in finding unpleasant. "What's all this about a plot about Dally?" he asked.

II

"You got that, Reg?" Dalessio asked. "If you get any more interference on this circuit, put it back on plain speech straight away. Then they can see how they like that. I don't believe for a bloody moment the line's been relaid for a single bastard yard. Still, it's being ceased in a week or two, and it never was of the slightest importance, so

there's no real worry. Now, what about the gallant Poles?"
He spoke with a strong Glamorganshire accent diversified
by an occasional Italian vowel.

"They're still on here," Reg, the lineman-mechanic, said,
gesturing towards the test teleprinter. "Want to see 'em?"

"Yes, please. It's nearly time to switch 'em through to the
teleprinter room. We'll get that done before I go."

Reg bent to the keyboard of the machine and typed:

HOW U GETTING ON THERE READING ME OK KKKK

There was a humming pause while Reg scratched his
armpit and said: "Gone for a piss, I expect. . . . Ah, here
he is." In typical but inextinguishably eerie fashion the
teleprinter took on a life of its own, performed a carriage-
return, moved the glossy white paper up a couple of lines,
and typed:

4 CHRISTS SAKE QUIT BOTHERING ME NOT 2000 HRS
YET KKK

Dalessio, grinning to himself, shoved Reg out of the way
and typed:

CHIEF SIGNAL OFFICER BRITISH LIBERATION ARMY ERE
WATCH YR LANGUAGE MY MAN KKKK

The distant operator typed:

U GO AND   SCREW   YRSELF JACK SORRY I MEAN SIR

At this Dalessio went into roars of laughter, digging his
knuckle into one deep eye-socket and throwing back his
large dark head. It was exactly the kind of joke he liked
best. He rotated a little in the narrow aisle between the
banks of apparatus and test-panels, still laughing, while
Reg watched him with a slight smile. At last Dalessio
recovered and shouldered his way down to the phone at the
other end of the vehicle.

"Give me the teleprinter room, please. What? Who? All right, I'll speak to him. . . . Terminal Equipment, Dalessio here. Yes. Oh, really? It hasn't?" His voice changed completely, became that of a slightly unbalanced uncle commiserating with a disappointed child: "Now isn't that just too bad? Well, I do think that's hard lines. Just when you were all excited about it, too, eh?" Over his shoulder he squealed to Reg, in soprano parody of Thurston's educated tones: "Captain Thurston is tewwibly gwieved that he hasn't got his pwinter to the Poles yet. He's afwaid we've got some howwid scheme on over heah to depwive him of it. . . . All right, Thurston, I'll come over. Yes, now."

Reg smiled again and put a cigarette in his mouth, striking the match, from long habit, on the metal "No Smoking" notice tacked up over the ventilator.

"Give me one of those, Reg, I want to cool my nerves before I go into the beauty-parlour across the way. Thanks. Now listen: switch the Poles through to the teleprinter room at one minute to eight exactly, so that there's working communication at eight but not before. Do Thurston good to bite his nails for a few minutes. Put it through on number . . ."—his glance and forefinger went momentarily to a test-frame across the aisle—"number six. That's just been rewired. Ring up Teleprinters and tell 'em, will you? See you before I go off."

It was dark and cold outside and Dalessio shivered on his way over to the Signal Office. He tripped up on the cable which ran shin-high between a line of blue-and-white posts outside the entrance, and applied an unclean expression to the Adjutant, who had had this amenity provided in an attempt to dignify the working area. Inside the crowded, brilliantly lighted office, he was half-asphyxiated by the smoke from the stove and half-deafened by the thumping of date-stamps, the ringing of telephones, the enraged bark of one sergeant and the loud, tremulous singing of the other. A red-headed man was rushing about bawling "Emergency Ops for 17 Corps" in the accents of County Cork. Nobody took any notice of him: they had all dealt with far too many Emergency Ops messages in the last eight months.

Thurston was in his office, a small room partitioned off from the main one. The unit was occupying what had once been a Belgian military school and later an S.S. training establishment. This building had obviously formed part of the original barrack area, and Thurston often wondered what whim of the Adjutant's had located the offices and stores down here and the men's living-quarters in former offices and stores. The cubicle where Thurston spent so much of his time had no doubt been the abode of the cadet, and then *Unteroffizier*, in charge of barrack-room. He was fond of imagining the heavily built Walloons and high-cheeked Prussians who had slept in here, and had insisted on preserving as a historical document the chalked *Wir kommen zurück* on the plank wall. Like his predecessors, he fancied, he felt cut off from all the life going on just outside the partition, somehow isolated. "Alone, withouten any company," he used to quote to himself. He would laugh then, sometimes, and go on to think of the unique lavatory at the far end of the building, where the defecator was required to plant his feet on two metal plates, grasp two handles, and curve his body into the shape of a bow over a kind of trough.

He was not laughing now. His phone conversation with

Dalessio had convinced him, even more thoroughly than phone conversations with Dalessio commonly did, that the other despised him for his lack of technical knowledge and took advantage of it to irritate and humiliate him. He tried to reread a letter from one of the two married women in England with whom, besides his wife, he was corresponding, but the thought of seeing Dalessio still troubled him.

Actually seeing Dalessio troubled him even more. Not for the first time it occurred to him that Dalessio's long, matted hair, grease-spotted, cylindrical trouser-legs and ill-fitting battledress blouse were designed as an offensive burlesque of his own neat but irremediably civilian appearance. He was smoking, too, and Thurston himself was punctilious in observing inside his office the rule that prohibited smoking on duty until ten at night, but it was no use telling him to put it out. Dalessio, he felt, never obeyed orders unless it suited him. "Hallo, Thurston," he said amiably. "Not still having a baby about the Poles, I hope?"

"I don't think I ever was, was I? I just wanted to make sure what the position was."

"Oh, you wanted to make sure of that, did you? All right, then. It's quite simple. Physically, the circuit remains unchanged, of course. But, as you know, we have ways of providing extra circuits by means of electrical apparatus, notably by utilising the electron-radiating properties of the thermionic valve, or vacuum-tube. If a signal is applied to the grid . . ."

Thurston's phone rang and he picked it up gratefully. "Signalmaster?" said the voice of Brigadier the Lord Fawcett, the largest and sharpest thorn in the side of the entire Signals unit. "I want a special despatch-rider to go to Brussels for me. Will you send him round to my office for briefing in ten minutes?"

Thurston considered. Apart from its being over a hundred miles to Brussels, he suspected that the story told by previous special D.R.s who had been given this job was probably quite true: the purpose of the trip was to take in the Brigadier's soiled laundry and bring back the clean stuff, plus any wines, spirits and cigars that the Brigadier's Brussels agent, an R.A.S.C. colonel at the headquarters of the reserve Army Corps, might have got together for him. But he could hardly ask the Lord Fawcett to confirm this. Why was it that his army career seemed littered with such problems? "The regular D.R. run goes out at oh-five-hundred, sir," he said in a conciliatory tone. "Would that do instead, perhaps?"

"No, it certainly would not do instead. You have a man available, I take it?"

"Oh yes, sir." This was true. It was also true that the departure of this man with the dirty washing would necessitate another, who might have been driving all day, being got out of the section billet and condemned at best to a night on the Signal Office floor, more likely to a run half across Belgium in the small hours with a genuine message of some kind. "Yes, we have a man."

"Well, I'm afraid in that case I don't see your difficulty. Get him round to me right away, will you?"

"Very good, sir." There was never anything one could do.

"Who was that?" Dalessio asked when Thurston had rung off.

"Brigadier Fawcett," Thurston said unguardedly. But Dally probably didn't know about the laundry rumour. He had little to do with the despatch-rider sections.

"Oh, the washerwoman's friend. I heard a bit about that from Beech. Not on the old game again, is he? Sounded as if he wanted a special D.R. to me."

"Yes, he did." Thurston raised his voice: "Prosser!"

"Sir!" came from outside the partition.

"Ask Sergeant Baker to come and see me, will you?"

"Sir."

Dalessio's large pale face became serious. He pulled at his moustache. Eventually he said: "You're letting him have one, are you?" If asked his opinion of Thurston, he would have described him as a plausible bastard. His acquiescence in such matters as this, Dalessio would have added, was bloody typical.

"I can't do anything else."

"I would. There's nothing to it. Get God's Adjutant on the blower and complain. He's an ignorant bugger, we know, but I bet he'd take this up."

Thurston had tried this, only to be informed at length that the job of Signals was to give service to the Staff. Before he could tell Dalessio about it, Baker, the D.R. sergeant, arrived to be acquainted with the Lord Fawcett's desires. Thurston thought he detected a glance of protest and commiseration pass between the other two men. When Baker had gone, he turned on Dalessio almost savagely and said: "Now look, Dally, leaving aside the properties of the thermionic bleeding valve, would you kindly put me in the picture about this teleprinter to the Poles? Is it working or isn't it? Quite a bit of stuff has piled up for them and I've been holding it in the hope the line'll be through on time."

"No harm in hoping," Dalessio said. "I hope it'll be

working all right, too." He dropped his fag-end on the swept floor and trod on it.

"Is it working or is it not?" Thurston asked very loudly. His eyes wandered up and down the other's fat body, remembering how it had looked in a pair of shorts, doing physical training at the officers' training unit. It had proved incapable of the simplest tasks laid upon it, crumpling feebly in the forward-roll exercise, hanging like a crucified sack from the wall-bars, climbing by slow and ugly degrees over the vaulting-horse. Perhaps its owner had simply not felt like exerting it. That would have been bloody typical.

While Dalessio smiled at him, a knock came at the plywood door Thurston had had made for his cubicle. In response to the latter's bellow, the red-headed man came in. "Sergeant Fleming sent to tell you, sir," he said, "we're just after getting them Polish fellows on the printer. You'll be wanting me to start sending off the messages we have for them, will you, sir?"

Both Thurston and Dalessio looked up at the travelling-clock that stood on a high shelf in the corner. It said eight o'clock.

III

"That's just about all, gentlemen," the Colonel said. "Except for one last point. Now that our difficulties from the point of view of communication have been removed, and the whole show's going quite smoothly, there are other aspects of our work which need attention. This unit has certain traditions I want kept up. One of them, of course, is an absolutely hundred-per-cent degree of efficiency in all matters affecting the disposal of Signals traffic, from the time the In-Clerk signs for a message from the Staff to the time we get . . ."

He means the Out-Clerk, Thurston thought to himself. The little room where the officers, warrant-officers and senior N.C.O.s of the unit held their conferences was un-heated, and the Colonel was wearing his knee-length sheep-skin coat, another piece of merchandise supplied through the good offices of Jack Rowney in exchange, perhaps, for a few gallons of petrol or a couple of hundred cigarettes; Malone's men's cigarettes, probably. The coat, added to the C.O.'s platinum-blond hair and moustache, increased his resemblance to a polar bear. Thurston was in a good mood, having just received the letter which finally buttoned up arrangements for his forthcoming leave : four days with Denise in Oxford, and then a nice little run up to Town for five days with Margot. Just the job. He began compos-ing a nature note on the polar bear : "This animal, although of poor intelligence, possesses considerable cunning of a low order. It displays the utmost ferocity when men-aced in any way. It shows fantastic patience in pursuit of its prey, and a vindictiveness which . . ."

The Colonel was talking now about another tradition of his unit, its almost unparalleled soldier-like quality, its demonstration of the verity that a Signals formation *of any kind* was not a collection of down-at-heel scientists and long-haired mathematical wizards. Thurston reflected it was not for nothing that the Adjutant so frequently described himself as the Colonel's staff officer. Yes, there he was, Arctic fox or, if they had them, Arctic jackal, smiling in proprietary fashion at his chief's oratory. What a bunch they all were. Most of the higher-ranking ones had been lower-ranking officers in the Territorial Army during the

Thirties, the Colonel, for instance, a captain, the Adjutant a second-lieutenant. The war had given them responsibility and quick promotion, and their continued enjoyment of such privileges rested not on their own abilities, but on those of people who had arrived in the unit by a different route: Post Office engineers whipped in with a commission, older Regular soldiers promoted from the ranks, officers who had been the conscripts of 1940 and 1941. Yes, what a bunch. Thurston remembered the parting words of a former sergeant of his who had been posted home a few months previously: "Now I'm going I suppose I can say what I shouldn't. You never had a dog's bloody chance in this lot unless you'd been at North Midland Command with the Adj. and the C.O. And we all know it's the same in that Mess of yours. If you'd been in the T.A. like them you were a blue-eyed boy, otherwise you were done for from the start. It's all right, sir, everybody knows it. No need to deny it."

The exception to the rule, presumably, was Cleaver, now making what was no doubt a shorthand transcript of the Colonel's harangue. Thurston hated him as the Adjutant's blue-eyed boy and also for his silky fair hair, his Hitler Youth appearance and his thunderous laugh. His glance moved to Bentham, also busily writing. Bentham, too, fitted into the picture, as much as the Adjutant would let him, which was odd when compared with the attitude of other Regulars in the Mess. But Bentham had less individuality than they.

"So what I propose," the Colonel said, "is this. Beginning next week the Adjutant and I will be making a series of snap inspections of section barrack-rooms. Now I don't expect anything in the nature of spit-and-polish, of course. Just ordinary soldierly cleanliness and tidiness is all I want."

In other words, just ordinary spit-and-polish, Thurston thought, making a note for his sergeant on his pad just below the polar-bear *vignette*. He glanced up and saw Dalessio licking the flap of an envelope; it was his invariable practice to write letters during the Colonel's addresses, when once the serious business of line-communications had been got through. Had he heard what had just been said? It was unlikely.

The conference broke up soon afterwards and in the Mess ante-room, where a few officers had gathered for a drink before the evening meal, Thurston was confronted by an exuberant Adjutant who at once bought him a drink. "Well, Tom," he said, "I reckon that fixes things up nice and neat."

"I don't follow you, Bill."

"Step number one in cooking your friend Dally's goose. Step number two will be on Monday, oh-nine-thirty hours, when I take the Colonel round the line-maintenance billet. You know what we'll find there, don't you?"

Thurston stared blankly at the Adjutant, whose eyes were sparkling like those of a child who has been promised a treat. "I still don't get you, Bill."

"Use your loaf, Tommy. Dally's blokes' boudoir, can't you imagine what it'll be like? There'll be dirt enough in there to raise a crop of potatoes, fag-ends and pee-buckets all over the shop and the rest of it. The Colonel will eat Dally for his lunch when he sees it."

"Dally's got three days to get it cleaned up, though."

"He would have if he paid attention to what his Commanding Officer says. But I know bloody well he was writing a letter when that warning was given. Serves the bastard right, do you see? He'll be off to the mysterious East before you can turn round."

"How much does the Colonel know about this?"

"What I've told him."

"You don't really think it'll work, do you?"

"I know the old man. You don't, if you'll excuse my saying so."

"It's a lousy trick and you know it, Bill," Thurston said violently. "I think it's completely bloody."

"Not at all. An officer who's bolshie enough to ignore a C.O.'s order deserves all he gets," the Adjutant said, looking sententious. "Coming in?"

Still fuming, Thurston allowed himself to be led into the dining-room. The massive green-tiled stove was working well and the room was warm and cheerful. The house had belonged to the commandant of the Belgian military school. Its solid furniture and tenebrous landscape pictures had survived German occupation, though there was a large burn in the carpet that had been imputed, perhaps rightly, to the festivities of the *Schutz Staffel*. Jack Rowney, by importing photographs of popular entertainers, half-naked young women and the Commander-in-Chief, had done his best to document the Colonel's thesis that the Officers' Mess was also their home. The Adjutant, in excellent spirits, his hand on Thurston's shoulder, sent Corporal Gordon running for a bottle of burgundy. Then, before they sat down, he looked very closely at Thurston.

"Oh, and by the way, old boy," he said, a note of menace intensifying the quack in his voice, "you wouldn't think of tipping your friend Dally the wink about this little treat we've got lined up for him, would you? If you do, I'll

have your guts for garters." Laughing heartily, he dug
Thurston in the ribs and added : "Your leave's due at the
end of the month, isn't it ? Better watch out you don't make
yourself indispensable here. We might not be able to let you
go, do you see ?"

IV

Early on Monday Thurston was walking up from the
Signal Office towards the area where the men's barrack-
rooms were. He was going to find his batman and arrange
to be driven some twenty miles to the department of the
Advocate-General's branch which handled divorce. The
divorce in question was not his own, which would have to
wait until after the war, but that of his section cook, whose
wife had developed an immoderate fondness for R.A.F. and
U.S.A.A.F. personnel.

Thurston was thinking less about the cook's wife than
about the fateful inspection, scheduled to take place any
minute now. He realised he had timed things badly, but his
trip had only just become possible and he hoped to be out
of the area before the Colonel and the Adjutant finished
their task. He was keen to do this because the sight of a
triumphant Adjutant would be more than he could stand,
especially since his conscience was very uneasy about the
whole affair. There were all sorts of reasons why he should
have tipped Dalessio off about the inspection. The worst of
it was, as he had realised in bed last night, when it was too
late to do anything about it, that his irritation with Dalessio
over the matter of the Polish teleprinter had been a prime
cause of his keeping his mouth shut. He remembered
actually thinking more than once that a thorough shaking-
up would do Dalessio no harm, and that perhaps the son

of an Italian café-proprietor in Cascade, Glamorganshire, had certain disqualifications for the role of British regimental officer. He twisted up his face when he thought of this and started wondering just why it was that the Adjutant was persecuting Dalessio. Perhaps the latter's original offence had been his habit of doing bird-warbles while the Adjutant and Rowney listened to broadcast performances of *The Warsaw Concerto*, the Intermezzo from *Cavalleria Rusticana*, and other sub-classics dear to their hearts. Cheeping, trilling and twittering, occasionally gargling like a seagull, Dalessio had been told to shut up or get out and had done neither.

Thurston's way took him past the door of the notorious line-maintenance billet. There seemed to be nobody about. Then he was startled by the sudden manifestation of two soldiers carrying brooms and a bucket. One of them had once been in his section and had been transferred early that year to one of the cable sections, he had forgotten which one. "Good-morning, Maclean," he said.

The man addressed came sketchily to attention. "Morning, sir."

"Getting on all right in No. 1 Company?"

"Yes, thank you, sir, I like it fine."

"Good. What are you fellows up to so early in the morning?"

They looked at each other and the other man said: "Cleaning up, sir. Fatigue party, sir."

"I see; right, carry on."

Thurston soon found his batman, who agreed with some reluctance to the proposed trip and said he would see if he could get the jeep down to the signal office in ten minutes. The jeep was a bone of contention between Thurston and his batman, and the batman always won, in the sense that never in his life had he permitted Thurston to drive the jeep in his absence. He was within his rights, but Thurston often wished, as now, that he could be allowed a treat occasionally. He wished it more strongly when a jeep with no exhaust and with seven men in it came bouncing down the track from the No. 1 Company billet area. They were laughing and two of them were pretending to fight. The driver was a lance-corporal.

Suddenly the laughing and fighting stopped and the men assumed an unnatural sobriety. The reason for this was provided by the immediate emergence into view of the Colonel and the Adjutant, moving across Thurston's front.

They saw him at once; he hastily saluted and the Adjutant, as usual, returned the salute. His gaze met Thurston's under lowered brows and his lips were gathered in the fiercest scowl they were capable of.

Thurston waited till they were out of sight and hurried to the door of the line-maintenance billet. The place was deserted. Except in illustrations to Army manuals and the like, he had never seen such perfection of order and cleanliness. It was obviously the result of hours of devoted labour.

He leant against the door-post and began to laugh.

V

"I gather the plot against our pal Dally misfired somewhat," Bentham said in the Mess dining-room later that day.

Thurston looked up rather wearily. His jeep had broken down on the way back from the divorce expert and his return had been delayed for some hours. He had made part of the journey on the back of a motor-bike. Further, he had just read a unit order requiring him to make the jeep available at the Orderly Room the next morning. It wasn't his turn yet. The Adjutant had struck again.

"You know, I'm quite pleased," Bentham went on, lighting a cigarette and moving towards the stove where Thurston stood.

"Oh, so am I."

"You are? Now that's rather interesting. Surprising, even. I should have thought you'd be downcast."

Something in his tone made Thurston glance at him sharply and put down the unit order. Bentham was standing with his feet apart in an intent attitude. "Why should you think that, Ben?"

"I'll tell you. Glad of the opportunity. First of all I'll tell you why it misfired, if you don't already know. Because I tipped Dally off. Lent him some of my blokes and all, to get the place spick and span."

Thurston nodded, thinking of the two men he had seen outside the billet that morning. "I see."

"You do, do you? Good. Now I'll tell you why I did it. First of all, the Army's not the place for this kind of plotting and scheming. The job's too important. Secondly, I did it because I don't like seeing an able man taken down by a bunch of ignorant jumped-up so-called bloody gentlemen from the Territorial Army. Not that I hold any brief for Dalessio outside his technical abilities. As you know, I'm a Regular soldier and I disapprove most strongly of anything damn slovenly. It's part of my nature now and I don't mind either. But one glance at the Adj.'s face when he was telling me the form for this morning and I knew where my duty lay. I hope I always do. I do my best to play it his way as a rule for the sake of peace and quiet. But this business was different. Wasn't it?"

Thurston had lowered his gaze. "Yes, Ben."

"It came as a bit of a shock to me, you know, to find that Dalessio needed tipping off."

"How do you mean?"

"I mean that I'd have expected someone else to have told him already. I only heard about this last night. I was the only one here later on and I suppose the Adj. felt he had to tell someone. I should have thought by that time someone else would have let the cat out of the bag to Dally. You, for instance. You were in on this from the start, weren't you?"

Thurston said nothing.

"I've no doubt you have your excuses for not letting on. In spite of the fact that I've always understood you were the great one for pouring scorn on the Adj. and Rowney and Cleaver and the rest of that crowd. Yes, you could talk about them till you were black in the face, but when it came to doing something, talking where it would do some good, you kept your mouth shut. And, if I remember rightly, you were the one who used to stick up for Dally when the others were laying into him behind his back. You know what I think? I don't think you care tuppence. You don't care beyond talking, any road. I think you're really quite sold on the Adj.'s crowd, never mind what you say about them. Chew that over. And chew this over and all: I think you're a bastard, just like the rest of 'em. Tell that to your friend the Adjutant, Captain bloody Thurston."

Thurston stood there for some time after Bentham had gone, tearing up the unit order and throwing the pieces into the stove.

COURT OF INQUIRY

COURT OF INQUIRY

I

"You free for a bit this afternoon, Jock?" Major Raleigh asked me in the Mess ante-room one lunch-time in 1944.

"I think so, Major," I said. "Provided I can get away about half-three. I've got some line-tests laid on for then. What do you want me for, anyway?"

"Here, let me top that up for you, old boy." Raleigh seized a passing second-lieutenant by the elbow. "Ken, run and get my batman to bring me one of my bottles of Scotch, will you? Oh, and incidentally what's become of your vehicle tool-kit deficiency return? It was supposed to be on my desk by ten-hundred this morning. Explanation?"

During this and what followed it, I first briefly congratulated myself on being directly responsible to the C.O. (the most incurious officer in the whole unit) rather than coming under Raleigh's command. Then I wondered what was in store for me after lunch. Perhaps a visit to another binoculars establishment or camera warehouse the major had discovered. My alleged technical proficiency had made me in some demand for such expeditions. Finally I looked about me. The Mess occupied a Belgian provincial hotel and this was its lounge, a square room lined with burst leather-padded benches. Officers sat on them reading magazines. Only the fact that two or three of them were also drinking stopped the place looking like a barber's waiting-room. Outside it was raining a little.

The major returned, smiling deprecatingly and re-sembling more than ever a moustached choirboy in battle-dress. "Sorry about that," he said, "but you've got to keep them on their toes. Now about this business this afternoon. Young Archer's made another nonsense."

"What's he done this time?"

"Lost a charging-engine. Left it behind on the last move, and naturally when he sent a party back the natives had removed it. Or so the story goes. I reckon that sergeant of his—Parnell, isn't it?—held a wayside auction and flogged it for a case of brandy. Anyway, it's gone."

"Wait a minute, Major—wouldn't it have been one of those wee 1260-watt affairs that take about a fortnight to charge half a dozen batteries? The ones nobody ever uses?"

"I wouldn't go all the way with you there, old boy." The major rarely went all the way with anyone anywhere. Very often he went no distance at all.

"Aren't they obsolete?" I persisted. "And wouldn't I be right in thinking they're surplus too?"

"That's not the point. This one was on young Archer's charge. The Quartermaster has his signature. Ah, here we are. Give me your glass, Jock."

"Thanks . . . Well, where do I come into this, sir? Do I hold Archer for you while you beat him up, or what?"

The major smiled again, fixedly this time. "Good idea. Seriously, though, I've had just about enough of young

Archer. I want you to serve on the Court of Inquiry with me and Jack Rowney, if you will. In my office. I'll take you over after lunch."

The major's modes of operation within his Company were often inventive to the point of romanticism. But even for him this was a far-fetched creation. "Court of Inquiry? But couldn't we get this thing written off? There's surely no need . . ."

"I'd get someone else if I could, but everybody's got their hands full except you." He looked me in the eye, and since I knew him well I could see he was wondering whether to add something like: "How nice it must feel to be a mathe- matical wizard and live a life of leisure." Instead, he waved to someone behind me, called: "Hallo, Bill, you old chiseller," and went to greet the Adjutant, just arrived, presumably, on a goodwill mission from Unit H.Q. There was much I wanted to ask Raleigh, but now it would have to keep.

II

Lunch in the heavily panelled dining-room was served by three Belgian waitresses wearing grey dresses and starched aprons. Their ugliness was too extreme to be an effect of chance. Perhaps they had been selected by a burgo- magisterial committee as proof against the most licentious of soldiery. Such efforts would have been wasted. Libido burnt feebly in Raleigh's domain.

The meal was stew and diced vegetables followed by duff full of grape-pips. While he ate it the Adjutant, resplendent in a new Canadian battledress, chaffed Raleigh in the quacking voice which Archer was so good at imitating. I thought about Archer and one or two of his nonsenses.

The trailer nonsense had been a good instance of the bad luck he seemed to attract. The trailer had had a puncture on a long road convoy led by him and, since trailers carried no spare wheel, had clearly been unable to proceed farther. But if General Coles, commanding the 11th/17th Army Corps Group, was going to be able to communicate with his lower formations that evening it was as clearly essential that the convoy should proceed farther, and soon. With rather uncharacteristic acumen, Archer had had the trailer unloaded and then jacked up with both its wheels removed, reasoning that it would take very energetic intervention to steal the thing in that state. But someone did.

Then there had been the telephone-exchange-vehicle nonsense. On another convoy Archer had gone off without it, an action threatening similarly grave disservice to General Coles. Fortunately one of my sergeants, happening to watch Archer's wagon-train lumbering out, had gone and kicked out of bed the driver of the exchange vehicle, promising violence if his wheels were not turning inside ten minutes. A message by motor-bike to the head of the convoy, recommending a short halt, had done the rest. Taxing Archer with this afterwards, I wrung from him the admission that the dipsomaniacal Sergeant Parnell had been the culprit. He had been ordered to warn all drivers overnight, but half a bottle of *calvados*, plus the thought of the other half waiting in his tent, had impaired his efficiency.

"Why don't you sack that horrible lush of yours?" I had asked Archer in exasperation. "You must expect things like that to happen while he's around. Raleigh would get him posted for you like a shot."

"I can't do that," Archer had moaned, accentuating his habitual lost look. "Couldn't run the section without him."

"To hell, man; better have no sergeant at all than him. All he ever does is talk about India and cock things up."

"I'm not competent, Jock. He knows how to handle the blokes, you see."

That was typical. Archer was no less competent, or no more incompetent, than most of us, though with Raleigh, the Adjutant and Captain Rowney (the second-in-command of the Company) taking turns to dispute this with him, his chronic lack of confidence was hardly surprising. And it was obvious to me that his men loathed their sergeant, whereas Archer himself, thanks merely to his undeviating politeness to them on all occasions, was the only one of their immediate superiors whom they had any time for. Without their desire to give him personal support in return, anything might have happened every other day to General Coles' communications, even, conceivably, to the campaign as a whole. According to Raleigh and the Adjutant, that was perhaps the most wonderful thing of all about Signals : junior officers got as much responsibility as the red-tab boys. But not as much pay, I used to mutter, nor as much power.

III

The afternoon had turned out fine, and I said as much to the Adjutant as, his goodwill mission evidently completed, he passed me on the wooden veranda of the hotel and got into his jeep without a word. Soon Raleigh, carrying a short leather-covered cane and a pair of string-and-leather gloves, turned up and walked me across the cobbled street to his office, pausing only to exhort a driver, supine under the differential of a three-tonner, to get his hair cut.

Raleigh's office had the distinction of being housed in

an office. Pitted gilt lettering on the window advertised an anonymous society of mutual assurances. Archer had told me the other day how moved he had been, arriving there to be handed some distasteful errand or comradely rebuke, at the thought of the previous occupants in session, grouped blindfolded round a baize-covered table telling one another what good chaps they were.

He was in the outer room of the place now, sitting silently with the appalling Parnell among the clerks and orderlies. He looked more lost than usual, and younger than his twenty-one years, much too young to be deemed a competent officer. He was yawning a lot. I went up to him when the sergeant clerk called the major over to sign something.

"Look, Frank," I said in an undertone: "don't worry about this. This Court has no standing at all. Raleigh hasn't the powers to convene it; the Company's not on detachment. It's a complete farce—just a bit of sabre-rattling."

"Yes, I know," he said. "Can I see you afterwards, Jock?"

"I'll come over to your section." The line-tests could wait.

I went into the inner room, a long low affair lit by a single window and an unshaded bulb that pulsed slowly. Rowney stood up and swept me a bow. "Ah, Captain D. A. Watson, Royal Signals, in person," he fluted. "Nice of you to look us up."

"I always like to see how you administrators live."

"Better than you long-haired scientists, I'll be bound."

"Materially, perhaps. Spiritually, no." It was hard not to talk like this to Rowney.

"Och aye, mon, ye're maybe nae sae far frae the truth."

"Shall we get on, chaps?" the major asked in his on-parade voice. "Don't want to be all night over this." He opened a file and nodded to me. "Get Parnell in, will you?"

I got Parnell in. He smelt hardly at all of drink. He proceeded to give an oral rendering of his earlier written report: Raleigh had passed me a copy. At the relevant time he, Parnell, had been explaining the convoy's route to the drivers. Then he had got into the cab of his usual lorry (the one carrying the cookhouse stuff, no doubt). Then they had moved off. Soon after arrival at the other end, Mr. Archer had said the charging-engine was missing and he, Parnell, must go back for it. Going back for it and return-ing empty-handed had taken eleven hours. In reply to questions, Parnell said yes, he had looked in the right place; no, nobody had been hanging about there; no, neither he nor, as far as he knew, anyone else had been detailed to look after the charging-engine; and yes, he would wait outside.

Archer came in and probably did his best to salute the Court smartly. The effort forced you to notice how badly he did it. He started on a rigmarole similar to Parnell's, then stopped abruptly and gazed at the major. "Look, sir," he said, biting his lips. "Can I put this quite simply?"

Raleigh frowned. "How do you mean, Frank?"

"I mean I lost the charging-engine and that's all there is to it. I should have made sure it was put on board and didn't. I just forgot. I should have gone round afterwards and had a look to make sure we'd left nothing behind. But I forgot. It's as simple as that. Just a plain, straightforward case of negligence and inefficiency. And all I can say is I'm very sorry."

Rowney started to ask a question, but the major restrained him. "Go on, Frank," he said softly.

Archer seemed to be trembling. He said: "What makes me so ashamed is that I've let the Company down. Completely. And I don't see what I can do about it. There just isn't any way of putting it right. I don't know what to do. It's no use saying I'm sorry, I know that. I'll pay for the thing, if you like. So much a month. Would that help at all? God, I am a fool."

By this time he was shaking a good deal and throwing his hands about. I wondered very much whether he was going to cry. When he paused, blushing violently, I glanced at the other members of the Court. The head of the second-in-command was bent over the paper-fastener he was playing with, but Raleigh was staring hard at Archer, and on his face was a blush that seemed to answer Archer's own. At that moment they looked, despite Raleigh's farcical moustache, equally young and very alike. I felt my eyes widen. Was that it? Did Raleigh enjoy humiliating Archer for looking young and unsure of himself because he too at one time had been humiliated for the same reason? Hardly, for Raleigh was not enjoying himself now; of that I was certain.

Still holding his gaze, Archer burst out: "I'm so sorry to have let you down personally, Major Raleigh. That's what gets me, failing in my duty by you, sir. When you've always been so decent to me about everything, and backed me up, and . . . and encouraged me."

This last, at any rate, was a flagrant lie. Had it not been, Archer would not have been where he was now. And surely he must know he had lied.

The major turned his head away. "Any questions, Jack?"

"No thank you, Major."

"You, Jock?"

"No, sir."

The major nodded. With his head still averted, he said: "All right, thank you, Frank. Hang on a moment outside, will you? You can tell Parnell to get back to the section."

Archer saluted and was gone.

"Well, thanks a million for inviting me along to your little show, Major," Rowney said, stretching. "Plenty of the old drama, what? Strong supporting cast. And very ably produced, if I may say so."

Ignoring him, Raleigh turned to me. "Well, Jock, what do you think?"

"About what exactly, sir?"

"Come on, man, we want to get this thing wrapped up. What finding? You're the junior member and you give your views first."

I gave the more militarily relevant of my views and Rowney did the same. Within the next twenty seconds the Court had found that engine, charging, 1260-watt, one, on charge to Lieutenant F. N. Archer, Royal Signals, had been lost by that officer in circumstances indicating negligence. Lieutenant F. N. Archer, Royal Signals, was hereby reprimanded. So that was that.

After an expressionless Archer had been acquainted with the findings and had left, I stopped at the door to chat to Rowney. I had never much cared for him but I was grateful to him this afternoon for having, in his own way, given his opinion of the major's little show. Out of the corner of my eye I saw Raleigh crumple up the Court of

Inquiry documents and stuff them into his trouser-pocket.

Outside in the thin sunshine the three of us halted for a moment before dispersing. Raleigh's face took on a summarising expression, with raised eyebrows and lifted lower lip. "If only he'd pull himself together," he said. "But . . ."

IV

In Archer's section office and store, surrounded by piles of camouflage nets and anti-gas clothing, I apologised to him for having been a member of the Court. He sat inattentively on a crate containing a spare teleprinter, finally rousing himself to take a cigarette off me and to say: "Funny thing about that charging-engine, you know. One of the things about it was that it wouldn't go. It never had gone in living memory. And then the tool-kit was missing. And no spare parts. And it was obsolete anyway, so it was not use indenting for spares. So it never would have gone."

"Did you tell Raleigh that?"

"Yes. He said it was irrelevant."

"I see."

"Another funny thing was that the Quartermaster's got one nobody wants in his store. Surplus. In running order. With tools. And a complete set of spares. The Q.M. offered it me."

"Did Raleigh say that was irrelevant, too?"

"Yes. It wasn't the one I'd lost, you see. Oh, thanks very much, Corporal Martin, that's extremely kind of you."

This was said to a member of Archer's section who had carried in a mug of tea for him, though not, I noticed aggrievedly, one for me.

Somewhere overhead aircraft could be heard flying east-

ward. Archer sipped his tea for some time. Then he said:
"Not a bad act I put on, I thought, in front of that rag-
time bloody Court of Inquiry. Sorry, I know you couldn't
help being on it."

"An act, then, was it?"

"Of course, you owl. You didn't need to tell me the thing
had no standing. But I had to pretend that I thought it
had, don't you see?—and behave like a hysterical school-
girl."

Archer was a good mimic, I reflected, but it was perhaps
questionable whether any amount of ordinary acting talent
could have produced the blushes I had seen. On the other
hand, I had no way of knowing how deeply he had thrown
himself into the part.

"That was what Raleigh wanted," he went on. "If I'd
stood up for my rights or anything, he'd just have decided
to step up his little war of nerves in other ways. As it was
I think I even made him feel he'd gone too far. That crack
about him always backing me up was rich, I thought. Well,
we live and learn."

Archer no longer looked lost. Nor did he look particularly
young. It was true, I thought, that the Army would lick
anyone into shape. You could even say that it made a man
of you.

I SPY STRANGERS

I SPY STRANGERS

"DOING WHAT'S RIGHT, that's going to be the keynote of our policy. Honouring our obligations. Loyalty before self-interest. None of this letting our friends down when we think it's going to serve our turn. Not that it ever does in the end, of course, that type of thing. We can all see that from what happened pre-war. It was greed and selfishness got us into that mess. Anyway, coming down to details a bit now. First, Europe."

The Foreign Secretary, a tall young man whose schoolmasterly and rather slovenly air did not rob him of a certain impressiveness, glanced over at the tanned, neatly moustached face of the Opposition's spokesman on Defence questions. It was from this quarter that real difficulty was to be expected, not from the Foreign Affairs spokesman, let alone from the Leader of the Opposition. For a moment the Foreign Secretary quailed. More than one member of the Government, he knew, found his policies absurd or extravagant rather than extremist and would gladly see him humiliated. He knew too that other, less overtly political reasons for this attitude were widespread on both sides of the House (and in the Visitors' Gallery). The temptation

to play safe was strong. But he must resist it. He could not
have it said that he had covered up his real programme with
comfortable platitude. That was what They had always done.

"In Europe," he went steadily on, "we're going to go all
out for co-operation and friendship with the Soviet Union.
France too, naturally, but the state France is in these days,
it'll be a long time before she's ready to play her full part
in world affairs. It's obvious the lead's got to come from
ourselves and the Russians. So first of all we have a system
of guarantees of small countries, done between us. That is,
Britain and the Soviet Union get together and say they'll
clobber anyone who tries to walk into Austria and Czechoslovakia and Poland and Greece and Albania and all those
places. And really clobber him, not just notes and protests
and sanctions. We're not going to have it like it was last
time.

"Then there's self-determination. That means everybody's
got to have their own country and their own government.
Nobody under foreign domination. Now I'll just take one
example and show the type of thing I have in mind."

He took his one example. It was Poland, not because he
thought it was an example, good or bad, of anything in
particular, but because he had not long ago read a short
book on recent Polish history and, as was his habit, made
notes on it. These supplied him now with many an unfamiliar name and obscure fact, made him sound like a bit
of an expert on Poland, and by implication, he hoped, on
politics in general. After an account of post-1918 events in
Eastern Europe, he leant heavily on Poland's outmoded
system of land tenure, the anti-democratic utterances of its
government in exile and the Warsaw workers' resistance in
1939 and since.

He had got a lot of this off by heart and was able to look round the debating chamber. Two Opposition back-benchers were ostentatiously playing cards, conversations were muttering away here and there, and the Chancellor of the Exchequer was apparently asleep, but on the whole there seemed to be the right kind of semi-attentiveness. At least two people were taking everything in. They were the Speaker, whom the Foreign Secretary instinctively distrusted but of whose basic progressivism there could be little real doubt, and the Parliamentary Under-Secretary to the Home Office, whose brilliant brown eyes stared disconcertingly into his.

Did anything ever happen as it should? For months he had been wishing with all his heart that the Under-Secretary would look at him like that one day. But now that it seemed to have come about he felt none of the sudden joy and confidence he had expected. All he got was a jolt in the nerves which caused his mind to skip a groove or two, so that he found himself implying pretty unambiguously, in the next sentence he uttered, that the building of the Roznów Dam had been an act of irresponsible provocation justifying to the hilt the Russian invasion of Finland.

This evidently went unnoticed. The Foreign Secretary, judging his audience to be adequately softened up by abstruse information, modulated to an account, statistically supported, of German atrocities in Poland. This led to a more lyrical passage on the theme of Russo-Polish brotherhood in arms, followed by a carefully worded suggestion that Russia had earned the right to get things set up her way at her end of Europe. Next, a designedly short paragraph on the Americans, in which protestations of admiring gratitude—meant to fool nobody—introduced the message that to have fought for the liberation of a continent brought with it no automatic right to a say in its future, and that the sooner the Yanks realised this and cleared off back to their own half of the world the better for everyone.

There was some show of applause here on both sides of the House, and a voice from the Visitors' Gallery was heard to say that the fellow was talking a bit of sense at last. Mildly encouraged, trying not to look at the Under-Secretary to the Home Office, the Foreign Secretary turned to a fresh page of his notes. "Next, the Middle East," he said.

Immediate uproar broke out in all parts of the chamber. Those who had managed without apparent protest to sit through a deluge of information about the Silesian coal-fields found they could not contemplate further lessons on the break-up of the Ottoman Empire or, it might be, the average weekly take-home pay of the Egyptian *fellaheen*. The Prime Minister felt it his duty to intervene. "Turn it up, Hargy," he called. "You've had nearly twenty minutes now. Give the other lot a go, eh?"

The Foreign Secretary addressed the Speaker. "What do you say, Mr. Archer?"

"Well,"—the Speaker glanced to and fro—"I think we might split this up a bit, don't you? Sort of debate parts of it at a time? How much more stuff have you got there?"

"About as much again, sir."

There was a general groan and some shouts of "Shame!"

"Order, order," the Speaker said, blushing slightly. "I think if you don't mind, Hargreaves, we might hold the rest of your speech for now. Let's hear from Sergeant— sorry: I now call upon the Leader of the Opposition."

This personage, the left breast of whose uniform bore

several campaign-medal ribbons, turned and exchanged energetic whispers with his colleagues. After a time he stopped shaking his head violently and started nodding it feebly.

Like many another political leader, he owed his position less to talent or even ambition than to a group of deficiencies: lack of general unpopularity, of immoderate enthusiasms, of firm views about anything. Sergeant Fleming helped his officers without taking their part in their absence, fiddled the stores inventory but not the leave roster, never stood the Company Quartermaster-Sergeant more than one extra drink an evening, helped to carry his passed-out mates to their billets and then dropped them on the floor. A natural middle-of-the-road man, Fleming, and equally naturally a Tory through and through, or perhaps just through. Nobody had thought of questioning his nomination as titular head of the alternative to a Government that extended, Popular Front fashion, from the Trotskyist at the Colonial Office to the Moral Rearmament International Christian Democrat who had found himself Chancellor of the Duchy of Lancaster.

Fleming's head was nodding faster now, though no less feebly, in fact slightly more so. He got up and said loudly and indistinctly: "Well, we've heard what my learned friend, that is the Foreign Secretary, what he's had to say about what he thinks ought to be done about foreign countries and that. And I must say I've never heard such a load of rubbish in all my born days. It beats me that a so-called educated man with all his intelligence can talk all that rubbish. What do we care about all these Poles and French? They let us down, didn't they? No, we've got to look after ourselves because there's nobody else will.

Break them all up into small states so's they can't start anything, that's the only way. Eh? All right, Bert. Well, I'm going to give you our military expert now because you've got to keep the peace, haven't you? That's the first thing, so I'll hand you over now to Sergeant Doll."

The military expert's military aspect was half misleading. He was in the Army all right, but the shape and condition of his moustache, the unnecessary presence round his waist of a splendidly furbished webbing belt, the very knot of his khaki necktie suggested the Officers' Mess at some exclusive armoured-car regiment of incessantly invoked lancer or hussar ancestry, rather than the Orderly Room at an unemployed half-unit of the Royal Corps of Signals. Doll's extreme efficiency behind the sergeant's desk in that Orderly Room was perhaps what had led him, in compensation, to adopt this heavily martial persona. If so, he would only have been acting out on an individual and more symbolic scale the compulsion (born of the inferiority feelings common to all technical troops) that had afflicted his superiors during the period of training in England. All present could very well remember the cross-country runs, the musketry competitions, the three-day infantry-tactics schemes with smoke-bombs and a real barrage, the twelve-mile route-marches in respirators which had seemed in retrospect to show such a curious power of inverted prophecy when the unit finally completed its role in the European theatre of war without having had to walk a step or fire a shot.

One of the most convinced proponents of these early rehearsals for death or glory was at the moment sitting in the Visitors' Gallery with a hard expression on his soft face. He was Major R. W. Raleigh, the commander of a communications company until just after the German surrender, and now, the bulk of the unit having departed to help furnish signal facilities at the Potsdam Conference, the overlord of a sort of dispirited rump. This, originally comprising most of his old company with the addition of a spare section from the cable-laying company, had been swollen by successive injections administered by higher authority. In the chaos of disbandments, postings, reformations and moves to the United Kingdom that characterised the aftermath of the campaign, a command like the major's represented a handy point of stabilisation, a nucleus for any sort of drifting particle.

Expansion, once begun, had been rapid. Daily erosions took place as a corporal with one set of qualifications or three signalmen with another suffered removal for eventual use in the Far East, but these were far more than redressed by reinforcements. At one time or another, and with or without warning, there had arrived a further cable-laying section that had proved superfluous at Potsdam, most of the small but variegated Signals formation lately serving a now-demolished independent parachute regiment, half a Base company without any officers or sergeants, an entire technical-maintenance section without any transport or stores, and two or three dozen teleprinter-operators, lineman-mechanics, drivers, electricians and fitters who had turned up individually or in little groups. All this amounted to a ration strength of something like twelve officers and four hundred other ranks, a total quite impressive enough to justify such gestures as renaming the original company office the Orderly Room and starting to refer to Sergeant Doll, the chief clerk in that office, as the Orderly Room Sergeant.

The major thought of Doll as a useful lad, and never

more so than this evening. A certain amount of undisci-
plined behaviour, of affected intellectual nonsense, even of
actual hints of disloyalty to the country—these were to be
expected of a mock parliament, but there was surely no
need for the thing to turn out quite so mock as it had.
The blokes seemed to think that they could simply get up
and say whatever they liked. Where that sort of attitude
got you had been made all too clear at the previous sitting,
when the bunch of jokers who called themselves the
Government had brought in their Nationalisation Bill. This
meant, apparently, that they were in favour of collaring
the coalmines, the steel industry, transport, public services
—everything that created wealth and employment—and
running them as they saw fit. That could never happen in
the real world, in England, but the major could not agree
with his friends in the Officers' Mess that the passing of
that Bill merely showed how idiotic the whole issue had
become—he wished he could. No, it was far more serious
than that: the indication of a really ugly mood. He had
too much sense of responsibility not to have come along
tonight to keep an eye on things, use his influence to stop
them getting out of hand. He hoped he would not have
to intervene. It would not be necessary if Doll did his stuff
properly, and Doll surely would. Reliable fellow, Doll,
even if he was a bit of a puzzle. That perpetual parade-
ground appearance and manner—what was it all in aid of?

Whatever the complications of Doll's internal drives, he
was not a middle-of-the-road man; indeed, to extend the
image a trifle, he was brushing up against the wall on the
right-hand side. In the melodious voice that had served him
so well as Complaints Supervisor at a large store in Leeds,
he was saying : "I shan't waste much time in destroying the

dangerous nonsense we've just been exposed to. Russia has always been an aggressive power and always will be unless we stop her. All that restrained the Reds until 1939 was weakness. Then they went for the Baltic republics, Poland, Finland, plus various Balkan adventures. Their only interest in self-determination is to prevent it. Desertions to the Nazis included . . . I beg your pardon?"

"Facts!" the Foreign Secretary was shouting above the Speaker's half-hearted appeals for order. "This is all just . . . insinuation. You haven't——"

"Facts?" The spokesman on Defence questions brought out his own notebook, then went on as mellifluously as before: "All right, facts. From *The Times* of June 29th. Czechoslovakia signed Ruthenia over to Russia. Why? Because the Czechs wanted to get rid of it? From a B.B.C. broadcast this morning. Russia is putting pressure on Turkey to revise their Black Sea Straits treaty and cede two territories to her. Why? Because the Turks are planning to blockade her? From another broadcast. Three hundred more Poles shot by the order of People's——"

"They were traitors, collaborators, there've been——"

"I've no doubt many of them were. But we shall never know now, shall we? These people should have been tried by an international court, as we've said we——"

"It was the heat of the moment. You always get——"

"As I started to tell you, these were executions carried out under sentences passed by People's Courts, there wasn't just a mob blazing away in the streets. But I really must appeal to you, Mr. Speaker, to quell these interruptions. I managed to keep quiet while all that Red propaganda was going on, so I don't see why——"

"All right, Sergeant Doll. Hargreaves, I must warn you

to keep quiet." There was reluctance and a half-buried
sympathy in the Speaker's tone.

"Sorry, sir. But I've simply got to ask him about the
Polish elections. Surely that proves——"

"*Order*, Hargreaves. You'll have to shut up or leave."

"Yes, sir."

The House resettled itself rather sulkily, feeling, and
muttering, that it was always the bloody same : the moment
you got a decent row going, some pernickety sod piped
up with some moan about order. Might as well be sitting
in the billet reading last week's paper.

"Thank you, Mr. Speaker." Doll stared across at Hargreaves. "As a matter of fact I welcome the opportunity
of saying something about those elections. I find it rather
odd that the Reds should be so keen to get those elections
held at this stage, with the country still in turmoil—but
then it'll be all right really, won't it?—with the Reds everywhere to see fair play. No undemocratic interference from
us or the French or the Yanks that might result in free
elections, because the wrong people might get elected then,
mightn't they? Can't have that, can we? Comrade Stalin
wouldn't like that.

"I should like to round off this question with a few
words on the Warsaw rising and the Reds' unfortunate
inability to come to the aid of their Polish brothers in arms.
In the spring of this year——"

Hargreaves had lost all the poise that might have been
expected of a Foreign Secretary, even a mock one. He
leant forward on the heavy, scarred wooden bench and put
his head in his hands. If only he knew more and could
think faster; if only he had at his side, as living proof that
Doll was wrong, one or other of the fine men and women

he knew on his local Labour Party branch committee, people who had grown up in the service of Socialism and given it all their spare energy, fighting in Spain, leading hunger marches, canvassing in hopelessly impregnable Tory strongholds. . . . He tried not to think of all that going to waste, failing ever to find its way to power. His almost continuous excitement over the results of the British General Election, due to be announced the following week, froze momentarily into despair. Contrary to what everyone thought he had never been a member of the Communist Party. He was suspicious of the one-party system and his doubts about the Russian labour camps still lingered. But if Doll's ideas carried the day at home there was only one logical step to take. Hargreaves was enough of a Marxist to recognise a situation in which the Left must combine against the main enemy. To have taken this half-decision brought him no relief : on tonight's showing he was politically useless.

His obvious dejection was not lost on Major Raleigh, whose soft face had softened somewhat since Doll began to put things in the right perspective and who was now leaning back in his chair in search of what degree of comfort it could provide. This was not great. Like everything else in the room it seemed to have been made without reference to human use. Typical German unimaginativeness, the major thought to himself. The small oblong windows, through which a strong late-evening sun was pouring, were set too high in the wall to be properly seen out of, certainly by most of the children who until recently had attended prayers here, sung Nazi songs or whatever it was they did in their school hall. Two rows of flat-topped desks had been dragged out of an adjacent store-room to form the Government and Opposition front benches. It would have taken a long-torsoed boy or girl to work at one with any ease or even see fairly over it, and the design demonstrably called for a far shorter-legged man than the average mock parliamentarian currently in occupation.

The major brooded for a time upon Hargreaves and the many things that could be done with or to him to make him less all-embracingly unsatisfactory—failing which, some positive enactment of how the world in general felt about him would do him good. The things available to the major ranged from giving Hargreaves an extra duty for being un-shaven (any and every day would do) to getting him trans-ferred elsewhere. An influential contact in the relevant department at General H.Q. was in the habit of seeing to it that, to a large extent, the major was able to decide who should and who should not be posted out of his command. There was only one place where, after a brief break in the United Kingdom, Hargreaves would finally be sent: a very hot and distant place, full of stuff which would interest him and which, as a budding expert on world affairs, he could not afford not to know about.

In one of his rare moments of self-contemplation, brought on by slight uneasiness over the impending Election result, the major had started wondering about the morality of despatching jungleward anybody under his authority who had happened to annoy him. The moment had sped harm-lessly by when he remembered that, to an experienced and conscientious officer such as he trusted he was, men who annoyed him were certain to be, corresponded one-hundred-per-cent with, men who were bad soldiers. It did not worry him that he was thus filling the relevant units of South-East Asia Command with drunks, incompetents, homosexuals,

Communists, ration-vendors and madmen. His first duty was to the formation he led.

Thoughts of the Japanese campaign naturally led him to consider another person who was going the right way about getting to it soon. Lieutenant F. N. Archer, sometime defendant in a celebrated unconstitutional court of inquiry staged by the major in an only half-successful attempt to humiliate him, was now scowling openly at what Doll was saying. Archer sat in a tall ecclesiastical-looking throne affair, much carved with Gothic lettering, at the far end of the room from the Visitors' Gallery. This was no gallery, but a simple row of hard chairs at floor level. The real gallery over the oak doorway had not suited the major, who still resented Archer's original attempt to make him and his friends sit up there as if they were nothing to do with the proceedings. It had been just like Archer not to see that it was absurd to try and reproduce the House of Commons set-up in details like that. Not seeing the obvious was his speciality, as his regimental work showed. To have appointed him Speaker of this fandango had probably been a mistake, but then he was the one who was always showing off his political knowledge in the Mess. A fat lot that had amounted to.

His voice sounding hollow in the barely furnished room, Doll said: "But before that we must immediately negotiate a peace with Japan, while she still has some sort of military machine left. We're going to need every ship and plane and man they have. A settlement wouldn't be difficult. They're talking about peace already. Nobody really cares who owns these islands—it's the bases that count. And with a common enemy that'd soon sort itself out."

"What about the Chinese?" the Postmaster-General

asked. He was a corporal of despatch-riders from the para-chute formation, one of the few recent arrivals who had taken part in the parliament.

Doll never smiled, but cordiality enhanced his tones when he answered : "An excellent question. I think the Japs with their reduced bargaining-power could probably be bullied into making enough concessions to the Chinks to keep them quiet. Certainly the Yanks have got quite enough cash to bribe the Nationalist Chinks—Chiang's lot—into selling their little yellow souls. The Red Chinks are more of a problem, though they won't amount to much for a good while yet. I think there's a fair chance they could be bought off too, into some sort of tacit neutrality anyway.

"But the real problem is Europe. The thing there is to advance until we're stopped. We stop wherever they start shooting. And they won't do that for a bit. We push into Czechoslovakia and Hungary and the Balkans and southern Poland if we can get there, until we're stopped. Then we dig in. They can't have troops everywhere. Later on we straighten the line by agreement with the Reds. It's our only chance of saving any of these people—to fight on our side later, if necessary.

"We'll need troops for that, of course. To dig in and stay there. Demobilisation must be halted at once. Twenty-eight days' leave in the U.K. for everybody we can spare, then back on the job. No Yanks are going home if I have any-thing to do with it; they're all needed here. Re-form the French, Dutch, Belgian and Italian armies. And the Ger-mans, as many of those boys as we can get. It does seem a pity we spent so much energy killing so many of them, doesn't it? When if we'd gone in with them when they asked us in 1941 we'd have smashed the Reds between us by now? But we'll leave that for the time being. We'll have to put the Nazi Party back on its feet, by the way. They understand these things. Perhaps old Adolf will turn up from wherever he is and give us a hand. We could use him.

"Well, that's about it. Keep them nattering away in Potsdam as long as possible and move like hell meanwhile. I think it would probably work. Everybody's exhausted, but our manpower and resources are superior. What we almost certainly haven't got is the will. That's their strong suit. In conclusion, let me just say formally that in foreign affairs the first policy of my party is resistance to Communism."

Doll sat down, having finished his speech, a rare achievement in this chamber. There was a lot of applause, most of it based on close attention to what had been said. Nodding his head to the pair of gloomy subalterns who sat beside him, the major joined judicially in. He knew he was supposed to be impartial, but really there could be no question but that the whole thing was on the right lines, except perhaps for the bit about the Nazi Party, which was premature to say the least. His speculations why Doll had never put in for a commission were interrupted by the Foreign Secretary, who clattered to his feet and cleared his throat in a long bellow. Hargreaves's normally mottled face was flushed; parts of his scrubby hair stuck out horizontally; his chest rose and fell.

"Could I ask first of all," he said in a trembling voice, "if the Honourable Member imagines that any British Government would put the policy he outlines, put into effect the policy he outlines?"

Doll's stare was not unfriendly. "Oh no. That's to say almost certainly not. They'd be turned out as soon as the electorate realised what they'd let themselves in for. You'd be asking people to admit in effect that they'd been fighting on the wrong side, you see, and having their relatives killed doing it. And they're tired too. No, I'd say the chances——"

"Then what . . . what the hell . . .? I mean what's the point of—— ?"

"The point? The point of what we're doing as I see it is to work out what we think we *should* do, not what the Government we elect *probably will* do. If we're all just playing a guessing game, then I think I'm with you. You'll very likely get what you want, especially if the country's fool enough to elect those Socialist prigs. I only hope you enjoy it when you find out what it's really like."

"Mr. Speaker, sir," Hargreaves cried, and he was looking directly at Archer, "I never thought to sit in this House, which is a, which exists only with the traditions of that other House across the sea, sir, and hear an Honourable Member admit to an admiration for the Nazi Party, which has been responsible for so many dreadful crimes, and which, the German Army I mean, we've been fighting it all these years and now I hear this said, or perhaps he now wishes to——"

"I didn't admit to an admiration for the Nazi Party, and I would never do so. Their racial policy was against reason and their appeal was based on mass hysteria. No, I was only arguing that in a desperate situation like ours you need all the allies you can get, especially if they can organise and fight. That we all know the Nazis can do."

"No wonder you want the Nazis. You're an aggressor, you want to aggress—you want to attack the Russians. The people who've died in their millions to stop the Nazis from conquering the world—honestly, how insane can you——"

The Foreign Secretary's voice tailed off. The House was perfectly silent, crossing its fingers with the wish that no pernickety sod was going to invoke order. Doll said efficiently: "The Nazis could never have conquered the world. There were too few of them and they were confined to one country. The Reds are an international conspiracy. And my proposals were entirely defensive. What interests me is resistance to Communism, as I said, not an assault on it. It's too early for that, or too late. There's only been one assault on it in our lifetime, and it failed because we were too stupid to join in. And now perhaps somebody else might care to——"

"Fascist!" Hargreaves screamed. "The strong arm, that's the thing for you, isn't it? The jackboot. The good old truncheon. I know your sort, Doll. There are people like you in England, all over, in the bloody Empire, Africa and India, smooth as buggery in the club with the old brandy and soda and then off to break a strike or flog a wog or . . . You're all the same. And everybody who clapped you . . ." His unblinking glance swept the chamber, meeting the major's eyes for a moment. "Ought to be ashamed of yourselves. Black-and-Tan material. You're going to lose. You're on the side of death. History'll get you. Auden warned you but you never listened. I won't even sit in the same room with you."

Sincere emotion enforces a hearing. Hargreaves had almost reached the impressive exit doorway—no more than twenty years old but, to an English eye, redolent of weighty Teutonic mediaevalism—before comment and protest got properly going. Doll smoothed his abundant straight dark hair. Archer and the Parliamentary Under-Secretary to the

Home Office gazed with similar expressions after the retreating Hargreaves. The major blew his nose and tucked the pale tan silk handkerchief into the sleeve of his battle-dress blouse. His soft face concealed emotion at the hardly won memory (he did not care to blur with too much detail his faculty for making quick decisions) that Archer was Hargreaves's section officer and, as such, responsible for everything he did.

II

"Anything special for me this morning, Wilf?" Major Raleigh hung up his service-dress hat—which, in defiance of his own edict, he regularly wore with battledress—on the fist-sized bronze knob of the bookcase door. Behind the glass of this, apart from a couple of dozen battered books in a foreign language or two, there huddled a heap of painted china vases and ewers which the major thought might be eighteenth-century or nineteenth-century or one of those. He had collected them from various houses and shops in the area and sometimes wondered what to do with them.

Captain Cleaver looked listlessly at a pad on his table. "I don't think so, Major. There's the pay to collect."

"Get one of the cable wallahs to go. Time they did something to earn their living."

"Well, it's a trip, you know, Major."

"So much the better."

"No, I was thinking somebody might like to go. Get out of the place for a bit."

"Oh, I see what you mean. Go yourself if you like, Wilf."

"Well, actually I was hoping to look in at the Officers'

Shop if you're not going to need me here. That's in the opposite direction to the cashier."

"Ask that parachute chap, then, Pinch or Finch or whatever his name is. He's been looking a bit down in the mouth."

"Winch. Yes, he has, hasn't he? He must feel a bit of a fish out of water here. Nothing going on. It must have been a bit different at Arnhem. All that excitement. Pretty hectic too, though. I expect he misses that, don't you?"

"What?" The major, at his In tray, stared up over his reading-glasses. They made him look ineffectively studious, like a neglected schoolboy at a crammer's. "Misses what?"

"You know, the excitement and the big bangs and so on at Arnhem. I was asking you if you thought he was missing it."

"Who?"

"Winch, the parachute chap."

"How the hell should I know what he's missing and what he isn't missing? And he wasn't at Arnhem, I asked him. Got taken off the drop at the last minute because of dysentery."

"I understood him to say——"

"He wasn't on the Normandy drop, either."

"Well, he wouldn't have been, would he? Normandy was Sixth Airborne. Arnhem was First."

"Yes. Look, Wilf, if you're going to the Officers' Shop there are a couple of things you might pick up for me, if you would."

"Certainly, Major, of course." Cleaver turned to a fresh page of his pad, pleased at the chance of writing something down, and poised his pencil devotedly. "Now then, what can I do you for?"

"Half a dozen handkerchiefs, the silk ones. Don't seem to be able to get anything ironed round here. Three pairs of the lightweight socks, size eight shoe. Not the elastic tops. If there's only the elastic tops don't get anything. Ties? No, I'm all right for those."

The major appeared to fall into a muse. Cleaver said: "Anything else, Major?"

"Hold on, I'm thinking . . . These American shirts. Has he got any left, do you know?"

"Well, he's probably got some more in by this time. He said he was getting some more in."

"Make sure they're the same. The same as I'm wearing now. See? . . . You're not looking."

"I am, honestly, sir. I know the sort."

"Make sure the collar's the same. Get me three of them. Fifteen and a half neck."

"Right."

"Just a moment." The major fondled his throat, his blue eyes bulging as he tried to see what he was doing. "Better say sixteen to be on the safe side. I'll settle up with you when you see what you've got, okay?"

"Right, Major. Oh, by the way, I meant to tell you——"

"What?"

"A message came over the blower from Movement Control in Hildesfeld. Just an advance warning—there'll be a teleprint through this afternoon with all the griff. A platoon of the Montgomeryshire Light Infantry are moving into the area some time tomorrow and we're to help them find accommodation. They were supposed to be doing guard duty at one of the D.P. camps, but it closed down a couple of days ago and so there's nowhere for them to——"

"But it's not our responsibility to fix them up. They're

not Signals." Raleigh spoke with an anxious severity, as if, conceivably, the platoon referred to might turn out to be the one in which someone very dangerous to him was serving, someone who had seen him cheating at picquet or torturing a prisoner.

"I know, but that's not what they're on about. These people will come under the Admin. Company in the ordinary way. It's just that—well, the Staff Captain in Hildesfeld seemed to think that with our knowledge of the area we could be pretty useful to these M.L.I. types. Know where to look and save them time. Just lend them an officer and a sergeant for a day or so. Nobody at Movement Control who'd do and if there were they couldn't spare him. They're run off their feet there."

The major hardly heard the last part of this. In the weeks since the war ended, even more since the larger part of the unit had gone to Potsdam, he had been possessed and tormented by dreams of triumph, renown or at least advancement. One of these, which he never visualised with full conscious attention, was about a local Nazi uprising crushed by him in a single prompt and ruthless blow. Another, disguised as an unuttered joke, involved the removal with ignominy of the C.O. as a chief executive of communications at Potsdam and the immediate substitution of himself: "Where's Raleigh? Get hold of Raleigh. There's only one man for this job and that's Dick Raleigh."

Dreams three and four engaged him more continuously, if less profoundly. Three he had taken what steps he could to bring to life. In the last month he had written three demi-official memoranda to the Signals general at Army Group headquarters. Their theme was that, if the war against Japan lasted long enough, there would probably be a role in it for a new full-dress Headquarters Signals unit, and that the body of troops at present under his command, admittedly miscellaneous but in a high state of training, could with advantage be used as the basis of such a unit. He himself, he had pleaded, could ask for nothing better than to stay on in uniform past the date of his expected release, indeed indefinitely, if he could be allowed to serve as its leader.

The first memorandum had been acknowledged with the utmost formality, the others not at all. As each day brought no word from Army Group H.Q., and as news of Japanese reverses mounted, the major fell back increasingly on his fourth dream. This had been put into his head by the compulsions of military geography. The medium-sized village in which he and his men were living had turned out to lie within administrative reach of a smallish but important railhead—the one at Hildesfeld. The Movement Control people there were faced with the task of propelling personnel westward about three times faster than their resources allowed. The accumulating residue had to be put somewhere. The major's village and its environs were an obvious lodgment for it. The major had taken it upon himself to provide communications between the railhead and the tankless tank troops, the gunless artillery sections, the reconnaissance detachments with nothing in Europe left to reconnoitre—all those whom destiny or administrative whim had transmitted in this general direction.

If this situation continued, authority would have to recognise it. A different type of man from the major might have noticed an analogy with the experiences of an ex-colonial territory on the threshold of statehood. As things were he simply saw himself as an Area Commandant with a lieutenant-colonelcy to match. Only one officer of this rank was known to be living hereabouts, a youthful Engineer on twenty-four-hour warning of departure who was rumoured to divide his time between drinking schnapps in a farmhouse bedroom and driving round the countryside looking for more, this at a speed which suggested that death might remove him before officialdom could. Of the five or six local majors, inquiry showed that Raleigh was senior to three and had been around the place longer than any. "Lieut-Col. R. W. Raleigh, R. Sigs" sounded authentic. So did "Winkworth (West) Conservative Association—*Chairman*: Colonel Richard W. Raleigh."

"All right, Wilf," the major said. "I'll take care of it. Was there anything else?"

"About the Shop again, sir. I take it it would be all right to get a few things for one or two of the blokes while I'm there?"

The major frowned. It was his major's frown, his responsibility-invoking frown, his slackness-detecting frown, his extra-duty-donating frown. He kept it on full for a while before he said: "I'm not sure that's a very good idea."

"Oh, I don't see why not. Things are pretty relaxed these days. We're not at war any more, after all. I can't see it doing anybody much harm."

"I wouldn't go all the way with you there, old boy. While the blokes have got so much time on their hands it's particularly important to maintain discipline. It doesn't help at all, throwing shoes and ties and what-not around indiscriminately. This is an Officers' Shop we're talking about, not a natty gents' tailoring establishment. Why do you think officers and men are required to dress differently?

To emphasise the difference in their status, of course. That's quite fundamental."

"I know, Major"—Cleaver was being uncharacteristically persistent—"but it's going on all over the place, you see. Only yesterday I saw a couple of the lads on the switchboard wearing those jeep coats, the sort with the———"

"They're in Archer's lot; I've already had a word with him about it. There's a great deal too much of this all-chums-together spirit around these days and I don't like it. It isn't . . . healthy. Anyway, who were you thinking of getting stuff for?"

"Well, evidently Doll could do with a couple of shirts, and the Quartermaster-Sergeant was talking about a few pairs of shoes—he didn't say who he wanted them for—and then my batman was asking———"

The major's frown, which had almost cleared, came back again, but with a difference that indicated that thought of some description was going on behind it. "That's rather different. Doll knows this sort of thing is a privilege and he's not the kind of fellow to abuse it. The Q.M.S. has done a first-class job for everybody at a very difficult time,"—and, the major might have added, a five-star *cordon bleu* crossed-knife-and-fork-in-the-Michelin-guide-type job for himself out of the petrol-hunger of a chain of civilians that stretched back as far as Arromanches on the Norman coast —"and if he needs a pair of shoes or two I don't think it's really up to us to question it. As regards your batman— well, I regard that as a personal matter between the two of you. Batmen have always had these little perks—it's a tradition. Yes, that's all right, Wilf."

"Thanks, Major."

"You did quite right to tell me, though," Raleigh said emphatically, leaving the other in no doubt about its being quite wrong not to tell him in the future, and picked up a sheaf of vehicle returns. He knew full well what was on them, for the transport situation, like much else, had remained static for weeks, but the small effort involved in putting common knowledge into due form helped to keep the sections on their toes, or at any rate off their backsides.

Cleaver cranked his telephone and after a moment said: "Parachute Section, please . . . What? When was this? I see. Is anyone working on it? Well, let me know the moment it's back, will you?—I say, Major."

Raleigh looked up as if he had been deep in the vehicle returns for a day or so. "What is it?"

"The line to the parachute people's out. Looks as if I'll have to go and tell Winch myself."

"Winch?"

"About the pay. We decided——"

"Yes, yes. Get Doll to send someone over. It's only a few hundred yards."

While Cleaver again cranked his phone and spoke, the major turned over his In tray a second time, then got going on his own phone. "Give me the Signalmaster . . . Signalmaster? Signals Command Group here, Major Raleigh. Who is that?"

"Archer, sir."

"Frank, what's happened to the morning summary of communications? It's supposed to be on my desk at nine o'clock."

Seated at his trestle table in the commodious and airy barn that housed the Signal Office, Archer blushed. "I sent it across, sir. Nearly two hours ago."

This inadvertent reminder of how long after nine o'clock the major had presumptively begun his morning's work did not go down well. "I don't care how long ago you think you sent it across, Frank, it isn't here."

"There's only one thing on it, sir—the line to Para-Sec is down; otherwise——"

"I know that. That's not the point. You'd better have a look round there and then come over and talk to me about it. I want a word with you anyway."

Sighing, Archer got to his feet and stretched. Inactivity reigned about him. A single teleprinter clattered away in one corner. A bespectacled corporal read a paperback novel in front of the wood-and-canvas rack in which transmitted messages were filed. The rack had been cleared at midnight and now carried half a dozen exiguous batches of flimsy. The two counter-clerks were playing chess while the orderly, an aged and delinquent Highland infantry-man, watched them in wonder. The locations clerk was busy with his eraser, removing what must have been one of the last official traces of yet another defunct unit.

Archer raised his voice. "Hargreaves!"

Peering anxiously, laboriously pinching out a cigarette, Hargreaves hurried in from the open air. His battledress blouse, instead of lying open at the top to reveal a collar and tie, was buttoned up and hooked at the throat; he must have been one of the last men in the British Army to avail himself of the recent sartorial concession. No doubt the older style made fewer demands on his time and energy. "Yes, Mr. Archer?" he said.

"You took the summary of communications across to Command Group, didn't you?"

"The what, Mr. Archer?"

"That thing I gave you to take over to the major's office, you took it, didn't you?"

"Oh yes. Captain Cleaver was there and I gave it to him."

"You're sure?"

"Oh absolutely, Mr. Archer."

"You'd swear to that?" Archer smiled conspiratorially. "They're trying to make out over there that I never sent it. You'd stand by me if it came to a court-martial, wouldn't you?"

Hargreaves looked worried. "I don't quite understand, Mr. Archer, but if there's any trouble you can count on me to——"

"Never mind, Hargreaves, I was only pulling your leg. . . . Good show you put up last night at the parliament, by the way—I was meaning to tell you."

"Oh, thank you very much, Mr. Archer, how kind of you. . . . You don't think perhaps it was a bit . . . extreme? You know, at the end."

"Not a bit, you were quite justified. These people need to be talked to straight once in a while. You keep at it. Oh, and I thought that bit about Auden came in very well. I didn't know you were a fan of his."

"I've just read a few of his things, sir."

"I see." Archer became conscious that he had been smiling rather a lot. "Right, that's all, Hargreaves, thank you."

"Thank you, sir."

On Archer's table lay a letter he had been writing to a friend of his in Oxford, one who, like most of his contemporaries, was medically unfit for military service—a doubly fortunate shortcoming in the present case, for one of this friend's several neuroses forbade him to be ordered about. The letter was full of undetailed assertions of hatred and misery, unsolicited news about what Archer's two girl-friends in England had been writing to him, and inquiries about issues of jazz records. He put on top of it the Signal-master's Diary—its sole entry for the morning read *0840 On duty F. N. Archer Lt.*—and told Sergeant Parnell, the superintendent, where he was going. Then he donned his ridiculous khaki beret and left.

Outside, the sunlight was intense. Hargreaves was stand-ing in the shade, leaning against the corner timber of the barn and talking to a switchboard-operator called Ham-mond, who among other things was Parliamentary Under-Secretary to the Home Office. He gave Archer an inquisitive brown-eyed glance.

Archer went down the yard, at one side of which a despatch-rider was dozing on a heap of straw, and crossed the cobbled street to the school building. He was thinking that the oddest thing about the major, or about himself, was that Raleigh's behaviour was getting funnier all the time without arousing any laughter in him, Archer. Take Raleigh's unconcealed delight whenever a new formation moved into the area and thus gave him another place to have a line run to and a telephone installed at, an amenity much resented by its beneficiaries, who would usually have spent most of the war too near a telephone and asked for nothing better than to remain incommunicable. The major had almost got drunk—he never did quite—on the strength of having foisted a special despatch run and *a wireless link* upon a Displaced Persons Area Authority on the verge of closure. He seemed very near believing that stuff like this represented a serious and adequate role for a group that had provided half the communications of an Army Corps Group headquarters at war; he no longer excused the farce of having a Signal Office here at all by saying (untruly) that it kept the lads busy.

The same shift of attitude had taken place over his road. This boulevard through the camp area, too short to matter except in terms of the energy its construction absorbed and totally unnecessary anyway because of the dry summer, was about to be extended to other parts of the major's tribal domain. Archer foresaw himself doing further stints of uninformed supervision, watching the hard-core and rubble go down, scouring the village for more wheel-barrows, driving out to the Engineers detachment to borrow yet more. Hitler had been funny too, but you had had to live in Valparaiso or somewhere to be able to laugh at him with conviction.

A flight of green-painted wooden steps led up the side of the school. Sergeant Doll was sitting on them, evidently improving his tan. With the affability of a pub landlord at the entry of a notable big spender, he called from a distance: "Good-morning to you, Mr. Archer, and how are you this fine morning, sir?"

"Oh, fed up," Archer said unguardedly.

"Well, I'm not, sir, I don't mind telling you." Doll made no move to get up and let Archer pass. "I've got plenty to eat and a decent bed and no work and nothing to spend my pay on and nobody to bother me. I'm winning, sir."

"Yes, you are, aren't you?" Archer, whose head was on a lower level than Doll's, noticed that the other seemed to have no hairs whatsoever in his nose. This had the effect of making his moustache appear, if not actually false, at any rate an isolated phenomenon.

"That was a nice little spot of bother at the old House of Commons last night, sir, wasn't it? Of course that fellow Hargreaves, he's unbalanced, isn't he? A lot of these Reds are, you know. There must be something in that particular philosophy that sort of attracts such people. He must be a perfect little darling to have in the section, Master Hargreaves. I don't know how you put up with him, sir, honestly I don't. I'd have got rid of him many moons ago."

"Oh, he's not as bad as all that. He is an educated man, after all."

"That makes it twenty times worse, sir, in my view. The corruption of the best is worst, I remember reading that somewhere. You'd be the one who'd know where it comes from, I expect, sir, wouldn't you?"

Archer looked up sharply, but Doll's eye was as bland as ever. "It's Latin," Archer said. "I think."

"No doubt, sir. It's really a pity Hargreaves made an exhibition of himself like that. Damaged his own case, I thought. Don't you agree, sir?"

There was a pause while Archer recalled what was perhaps his sole intelligently self-interested action since joining the Company: putting a half-bottle of whisky on Doll's desk last Christmas Eve. Ever since then the major, who tended to make a confidant of Doll, had found that his little surprises for Archer, in the shape of unheralded inspections of the Signal Office and the like, had an odd way of turning out not to be surprises after all. Rather late in the day, Archer was discovering a related principle, that the Army afforded unique scope for vindictiveness and that disagreement on apparently neutral matters often provoked such a reaction. He knew now that the Adjutant of the unit, who had of course gone to Potsdam with the others, had been that sort of person, selecting junior officers for troublesome duties less by caprice than by remembering who had most recently contested his opinion in the Mess, even if the subject had been literature or the weather. Sometimes a tendency to confuse names (surprising in so incessant an advocate of attention to detail) gave his selections an involuntary impartiality. After thinking about it for two years, Archer was nearly sure that a historic mission to collect a new type of line-transmission apparatus, entailing a journey three-quarters of the way across England and back in January and two successive nights in an unheated railway carriage, had fallen to his share because a second-lieutenant called Belcher, whom Archer hoped he did not in the least resemble, had a day or two earlier contradicted the Adjutant about *Alice in Wonderland*. But as the Adjutant got to know his subalterns better, such miscarriages of injustice had become rarer, not that this change had been to Archer's advantage.

Although Archer had never made any progress in finding out what Doll was like, he judged it unwise to risk diminishing the effect of that half-bottle by saying what he really felt about Hargreaves's outburst and thence, inevitably, what he felt about Doll's politics. The major's régime was doubtless drawing to a close, but its last days might well be marked by a fury of moral violence. Archer could not afford to irritate a friend at court, or anywhere else for that matter. He said decisively: "Yes, he did go too far, much too far. I think he feels a bit cheap about it today. You weren't annoyed, I hope?"

"Oh no, sir, my back is broad. As I say, all he did was help my side. That Government'll fall soon, you mark my words. You were wanting to see the major, sir, were you?"

"Yes, I thought I might look in."

"He's got Captain Cleaver with him at the moment . . . Ah, here is the captain now."

Doll got up as Cleaver emerged from the doorway and descended the steps. Archer grinned at him; Cleaver was the one officer in the detachment whom he regarded with nothing but contempt—groomed for stardom by the Adjutant and finally rejected on the grounds of technical incompetence : a tremendous achievement. He had got his captaincy, though. "Hallo, Wilf," Archer said.

"Oh, hallo," Cleaver said, getting into his tone surprise at being so familiarly addressed. He carried gloves and a short cane and looked more than ever like a British officer as pictured in a German army manual. "The major's waiting for you."

The major was looking out of the window. A cow wearing a large floppy hat had just run along part of his road (known to everyone but himself as Raleigh's Alley) and then turned off to flee up the lane past the wireless section's billet. From somewhere near at hand a loud silly laugh had floated into the air. Whether this was associated with the cow or not, the two manifestations combined to pique and depress the major. They formed for him a symbol of anarchy mounting, of discipline and seriousness and purpose melting away. He felt there was some connection here with the chance of a Labour victory at the polls. Apart from a few negligible wild men like Hargreaves and Archer, he had never met anyone who confessed to having cast his proxy vote for Labour. On a recent visit to the Mess at Hildesfeld he had made a pointing of questioning his hosts on the matter and had heard the same story. His wife's letters said that nobody knew of anybody in the

whole town who was a Labour supporter and that everybody felt very sorry for poor Mr. Jack, the Labour candidate. And yet the major was uneasy. Something monstrous
and indefinable was growing in strength, something hostile
to his accent and taste in clothes and modest directorship
and ambitions for his sons and redbrick house at Purley
with its back-garden tennis-court.

Somebody tapped on the door. The major called "Yes?"
and started speaking the moment Archer began crossing
the threshold—a valuable foil, this, to his normal keep-'em-
waiting procedure. "Now, Frank, where's the summary of
communications?"

Archer walked over to Cleaver's table and instantly
picked up a duplicated form in pale-blue ink with manuscript additions. "Here it is, sir."

The major took it and went back to his seat. On the
whole, he seemed mollified rather than the contrary. "About
this parliament business, Frank. I'm not at all happy about
it."

"I'm sorry to hear that, sir."

"I'm seriously thinking of closing it down."

"Surely there's no need for that?"

"That disgusting display of Hargreaves's last night.
Couldn't you have prevented it? After all, as Speaker you
must have some ... And as an officer, you——"

"I don't think that anything but force would have——"

"Worst thing in the world for discipline. If the blokes get
the idea that they can simply——"

"Oh, I don't agree at all, sir."

The major's eyes narrowed. "What?"

"It's a chance for them to let off steam, you see. They're
off parade—rank doesn't count in there. Everyone accepts

that. I mentioned last night to Doll just now and he obviously didn't resent it."

"That's not the point. And if rank doesn't count, why aren't officers and W.O.s allowed to take full part, instead of having to sit out like that? I let you have your way there, since you were organising the thing, but I never followed your argument."

"Well, sir, rank doesn't count there really, but chaps may think it does. They might feel chary of giving, er, let's say Wilf Cleaver a proper hammering when they wouldn't if it was a corporal from another section, or even their own."

"Mm. I don't think the blokes are quite as stupid as you make out."

Archer shrugged.

"Tell me, Frank, I've often wondered : why do you hang on to Hargreaves when you've had so many chances to get rid of him? Does the section no good all round, having a type like that in it. Bad for morale."

"I just feel ... he's more or less settled in there. He's not much liked, but at least he's tolerated. Anywhere else he'd probably have a much thinner time."

"But good God man, a Signals section doesn't exist to give a home to stray dogs and to wet-nurse people. It's supposed to be an efficient unit in a war machine."

"Hargreaves can't do the Allied cause much harm now."

"Perhaps I'd better remind you, Frank, that we're all still in uniform and that our country is still at war. We're not on holiday."

Standing before the major's table, Archer shrugged again and put his hands on his hips. His eye fell on a framed text that said : *Ich will mich freuen des Herrn und frölich sein in Gott.*

"Confidentially now, old boy, what's the matter with Hargreaves? Basically the matter?"

"That's very simple, sir. He doesn't like the Army."

The major laughed through his nose. "I should imagine very few of us would sooner be here than anywhere else. If a man isn't a cretin he knows it's a question of getting a job done. A very important job, I take it you agree?"

"Oh yes, sir. And Hargreaves is clear on that too. But it isn't being in the Army that gets him down. It's the Army."

"I'm afraid you're being too subtle for me, Frank."

"Well, as far as I can make him out—he's not an easy man to talk to, but the way he sees it, people have been nasty to him in the Army in a way they wouldn't be in civilian life. The Army puts power into the hands of chaps who've never had it before, not that sort of power, and they use it to inflict injustices on other chaps whom they happen to dislike for personal reasons. That's the way the Army works. According to Hargreaves."

"Don't stand like that, Frank," Raleigh said, and waited until Archer had removed his hands from his hips and put them behind his back. "Well, whatever friend Hargreaves feels about being in the Army, you can tell him from me to pull himself together. So far I've tried to keep the original Company in one piece as far as possible. When postings come through I've been seeing to it that they've got passed on to these new arrivals. But there's always plenty of call for blokes with Hargreaves's qualifications, or lack of them rather, and I can get him out of the way any time I want to. If there's one more bit of nonsense from him I'll see he's on the first available boat for Burma. Is that clear?"

"Yes, sir. I'll tell him."

"And what's going on between him and young Hammond?"

"Going on? Nothing that I know of. They are friends. Hammond's about the only chap Hargreaves talks to."

"Is that all he does to him? Talk?"

"I don't know what you're driving at, sir."

"Oh yes you do, Frank, don't you try and bullshit me. There's something pretty unsavoury about that friendship, as you call it, if half I hear is true."

"I'll go and fetch Hargreaves and Hammond now, sir, if you like, and you can fetch whoever's been telling you this and get him to repeat it in front of them. And me too, of course, as their Section Officer."

"There's no need to take that tone, old boy. I'm simply telling you as a friend to be on your guard. You don't want a scandal in the section, do you? Hammond's a good lad and I shouldn't like him to get into any sort of trouble. If things turn out the way they might I'd consider him favourably for lance-corporal. Well, I suppose you'd better be getting back to the Signal Office. Sorry to have kept you, but this Hargreaves business has been on my mind rather."

"Yes, sir."

"Oh, before you go, Frank, any news of *Journey's End*?"

"The librarian chap in Hildesfeld says he'll do his best, but it's been out of print for years. The British Drama League in England are on the job now, apparently."

"Good. I hope it comes through. It would be fun to have a shot at putting it on. Do you know it at all?"

"I'm afraid not, sir."

"It's good stuff, you know, Frank. You'd like it. The best thing on the first war by far. Really gets the spirit of the trenches, the feel of what it was like."

III

Major Raleigh stood on the steps of the farmhouse where the Officers' Mess was, trying to smell the lilac bushes. He was having a hard time of it. Competing smells included the one from the cookhouse bonfire, a mixture of rum and hot cardboard; the one from the henhouse where the Mess's looted chickens lived; the one from the piggery; the one from nowhere and everywhere that was apparently endemic to continental farmyards, about midway between that of a brewery and that of burning cheese-rind. As one of his own wireless operators might have tried to tune out interference, the major stopped and laid his soft nose alongside one of the pale clusters. It tickled, but he got something.

The voice of Cleaver spoke behind him. "Are you all right, Major?"

"Of course I'm all right," Raleigh said, wheeling round as he came upright.

"I'm sorry, I thought you were ill."

"Well I'm not. Are you ready?"

"Yes, Major. Nobody else seems to want to come."

"Did you ask them?"

"Yes, Major."

"All of them?"

"Yes, Major."

"It's a pity some of them couldn't have taken the trouble to come along," Raleigh said, voicing a desire for his brother-officers' company that was to cool sharply within the hour. "All right, Wilf, let's get moving. We're late already."

The two got into the major's car, a saloon with faded checkerboard painting on the radiator and a cracked mica windscreen. Its only superiority over the major's jeep lay in the latter vehicle's having reached the stage of needing to carry a can of petrol, a can of oil and a large can of water whenever it went anywhere. And this thing was a piece of loot, too. While he pulled at the starter and the motor lurched over, Raleigh imagined his friends at Potsdam, each in a Mercedes with the back full of cameras, watches, automatic pistols, pairs of binoculars, crates of champagne and vodka and American whiskey, haunches of venison. . . . Girls did not appear on the major's list; he considered that side of life much overrated. Before the car came shudderingly to life he had time for a surge of feeling, equally compounded of envy and righteous indignation, at the memory of a current rumour about a large R.A.F. Signals unit which, ordered to return to England with all its stores and transport, and thus secure against Customs inspection, had stuffed every cranny with cameras, watches, automatic pistols—perhaps girls.

They moved out of the yard, with a grinding bump when one of the rear mudguards, worse adjusted than its fellow, met the edge of the road surface. The sun was setting over the fields of rye or oats or barley or perhaps just wheat and there was arguably a fair amount of tranquillity and such about, but the major was beyond its reach. As he frequently said, it was people that interested him. The people interesting him at the moment were still the ones he knew at Potsdam. "Funny to think of them all up there," he said. "Bill and the C.O. and Jack Rowney and Tom Thurston and all that crowd. And Rylands and Ben and Dalessio and Jock Watson. Wonder what they're all up to. Parties with the Russians and the Yanks and God knows what. All the big brass-hats around. The Jerries too. And . . ."—the major tried briefly to visualise what more might be on view there than other soldiers—"everything. Of course I realise we couldn't all have gone, but I do wish——"

"The C.O. and the Adjutant tended to pick the crowd who'd been with them at North Midland Command."

"Yes, I know they did." A military Calvinist who had had demonstrated to him his own non-membership of the elect, Raleigh spoke in a neutral tone. "Not altogether, though. They took Dalessio with them."

"I wonder why."

"Rylands seemed to think Dalessio was indispensable," the major said. Then, quite as if he realised that this was not the most tactful thing to say to a man whom all sorts of pressure had failed to get into Dalessio's job, he added: "I wouldn't go all the way with him there."

"I hear Bill and Jack and Tom are all majors now."

"Yes. I'm particularly pleased Tom got his crown. He didn't fit in quite at first, I thought—bit of an awkward cuss. But some time last winter he pulled himself together and started doing a first-class job. Co-operated for all he was worth."

The car laboured up an incline past the burnt-out wreck of a civilian lorry, relic of the celebrations on V.E. night. The cuff of a *Wehrmacht* jacket, charred and faded, hung out of the remains of the cab. Raleigh was about to comment adversely on this memorial of indiscipline, or of high spirits, but changed his mind and said abruptly: "I'd give anything to be at Potsdam."

"I'd have thought we were better off here, Major, with the staff off our backs at last after two years."

"They're doing a job there, that's the difference. I suppose ... I suppose I might still get the chance of taking the

Company to the Far East. Depends how the war goes, partly." The major was thinking as usual in terms of a Headquarters Signals unit, not of a mere company, and of a lieutenant-colonelcy, but he was too shy to tell Cleaver this.

"I didn't realise you were as keen on the Army as all that, sir," Cleaver said carefully.

"Well, I've been doing a lot of thinking these last few weeks, Wilf. Serious thinking. First real chance I've had since 1939. I worked it out that I've spent half my adult life in the Army. Pretty shaking thought, that. I've got used to being in uniform. Hardly remember what it was like in Civvy Street. And from the way things are going it looks as if I might not care for it when I arrive there. If these Socialists get in——"

"I shouldn't worry too much, Major. However badly it turns out there's sure to be scope for, well, initiative and quick thinking and all the rest of it."

"I hope you're right."

The major parked the car in the Signal Office yard between an iron canister full of broken glass and a disused boiler stuffed with torn sheets. The two officers crossed the road to the school building and entered the hall.

Parliament was in session. As Raleigh led the way to the Visitors' Gallery, his shoes thudding on the greasy bare boards, an instrument-mechanic on the Government side was saying: "We're going to build a decent Britain. Fair shares for all and free schools and doctoring and hospitals and no class distinction. The old school tie and the old-boy network aren't going to work any more. To make sure of that we're going to abolish the public schools and Oxford and Cambridge, or at any rate change them so that anybody who's got the brains can go to them, and we're going to either abolish the House of Lords or make it a thing you vote on, just like the House of Commons. It's undemocratic any other way. Some of us want to abolish the Royal Family for the same reason, but we're not decided about that. Personally I think that if you scrap titles and the Honours List and all that carry-on, then you can leave the King and Queen to stew in their own juice."

The major's mouth tightened. So far he had refrained from interjecting more than a sentence or two into these debates, but after what he had just heard, and in this evening's intensified mood of discontent, he knew he would be failing in his duty to all sorts of entities—to common sense, to discipline both military and civil, to England, yes, and to the King, why be ashamed of it?—if he refrained from extensive comment. His eye met that of Cleaver, who looked away instantly. The major waited impatiently for the Home Secretary or whatever he was to finish.

Interest in the parliament had fallen off from the moment of its inception. Deliveries of newspapers and magazines had recently improved in speed and quantity and the major suspected that access to civilian drink had likewise improved; he must get his batman to keep his ears open. Less than half the original members were in their seats tonight. The Opposition front bench lacked its Leader and its spokesman on Defence questions: Doll had declared himself finally disgusted with his fellow-M.P.s' frivolity—"I think it's ridiculous spending a lot of your time and thought preparing stuff for a load of apes, sir, don't you?" The ministerial bench was even more thinly held, with the Lord Privy Seal (if the truth were known) risking court-martial by thoroughly fraternising with a nurse from the civilian hospital in Hildesfeld, the Chancellor of the Exchequer asleep on his bed with a three-day-old *Daily Express* over him, the Prime Minister himself with two of his mates from the Sergeants' Mess attacking something they vaguely thought of as gin in something they even more vaguely thought of as a pub on the far side of the railway yard. But the Foreign Secretary was in his seat, and the young man the major very precisely thought of as that official's boy friend was in his.

The Home Secretary might have been thought to be drawing to a close, although, as the major reminded himself, you could never tell about that or *anything else* with fellows as unused as this to public speaking or indeed to *anything else* even remotely to do with the highly responsible and specialised and difficult task of running a modern industrial state. "You heard the other week about how we're going to give the Empire back to the blokes that live there," the Home Secretary was saying : "well, we're going to do the same thing, so to speak, with Great Britain itself. The country belongs to the ordinary working bloke and by Christ he's going to be running things from now on. No messing."

The major brushed his moustache with his knuckle and looked at the cracked and scaled maps which, in the absence of anything else that might blot out some of the clay-coloured plaster, somebody had pulled out of a cupboard and hung up. What a mess Europe had evidently been in in 1555, with all those hundreds of little countries, quite different from today, and how big Naples and Venice had been then. The major remembered enough German to wonder how there could ever have been *two* Sicilies. And again, who was Van Diemen and how had he filled in his time in Tasmania?

"Good enough, then," the Home Secretary said. "There are just three principles involved here: liberty, equality and fraternity. You'll remember that that's what the French Revolution was about. Well, we're not going to have a revolution about it, that's not the way we do things in England, not violent revolutions anyway, with barricades and shooting and so on and so forth. But there's going to be a revolution nevertheless and nobody's going to stop us."

He sat down amid varied applause from his own side. The major looked at the Speaker for the first time and raised a finger in assumed humility. Archer seemed to pretend not to have seen him at first, then, having looked round the chamber, caught his eye and nodded to him.

"I shan't keep you long," the major said as he rose to his feet. "But there are just one or two points I feel I ought to put to you, if I may. We're all equal here—we're all members for Arromanches and Bayeux and Amiens and Brussels and Mechelen and Tilburg and Münster and Rheine and all the rest of the bloody places, and we can talk to each other as gentlemen. We've been through the whole thing together. And the first thing I want to say to you is this. Everybody's done a first-class job, you have and I hope we have as far as it was possible to us, and of course the fighting troops, nobody can say what they went through.... Anyway, sitting here tonight it just occurred to me that it would be an awful pity if we were to let one another down by forgetting the things that have made it all possible, the teamwork and sense of responsibility, and behind that the way of life we've been fighting for. We've always been a pretty good-natured lot, we British, and the fellow up here"—he raised his hand to shoulder level—"and the fellows down there"—he extended his arm downwards with the hand still spread—"have always got on pretty well together. Each has had his job to do——"

Hargreaves stood up and said: "I spy strangers." He spoke loudly but unemotionally, as if promulgating his occupation rather than delivering a challenge.

The major stopped speaking immediately and looked towards the Speaker with an expression of courteous bafflement.

The Speaker's expression was of incredulous horror. He said: "Er...Hargreaves...can't we...?"

"I spy strangers," Hargreaves repeated a little louder, gazing into space.

"Could I ask you to clarify that, Mr. Speaker, sir?" the major asked good-humouredly.

Archer replied as if the words were being wrung out of him. "I was reading...it's a formula calling for the expulsion of unauthorised persons from the debating chamber. The idea was——"

"Unauthorised persons?" Smiling, the major glanced from face to face. "But surely——"

"The thing is that officially only Members of Parliament are allowed to be present," Archer said, more steadily than before. "Anybody else is here on sufferance. *I spy strangers* is the way of saying you want to cancel that sufferance, so to speak."

Raleigh still smiled. "Are you ordering me to withdraw, Mr. Speaker?"

"I'm telling you what the book says."

In the pause that followed, the major again looked round the House, but nobody returned his look. He went on trying to think of something to say until it became clear to him that there was nothing to say. With a glance at Cleaver,

who quickly rose and followed him, Major Raleigh with-
drew.

Outside in the darkness he said : "You drive, Wilf, will
you? I want to think."

"Are you all right, Major?"

"Wilf, if you ask me if I'm all right once more I'll...
Anyway don't. Just shut up."

"Yes, sir."

IV

"Well, you must be pretty pleased, Mr. Archer, I expect,
at the way things have gone."

"Yes, I must admit I am, Sergeant. Such a thumping
majority, too."

"Yes, that did rather take me by surprise. I expected it to
be a much closer-run thing than this. Of course, being wise
after the event, it's not difficult to see what happened. The
Service vote did it. The lads have been in uniform all these
years and they've had enough. Voting Labour's a protest.
It's a way of saying you're browned off and want to go
home."

"Oh, there's a lot more to it than that, I'm quite sure.
People are browned off *with* something, or rather somebody,
a lot of somebodies. They're protesting *against*———"

"Well, you and I are never going to see eye to eye there,
sir, are we?—not even if we discuss it all night. We might
as well accept it."

"Will you join me in a glass of whisky, Sergeant? If it
doesn't seem too like drowning your sorrows while I celebrate."

"Thank you, sir, I will. You've certainly got something

to celebrate, and everybody else seems to be doing it, so I don't see why I shouldn't join in."

Doll and Archer sat in the little sitting-room—all painted screens and wax fruit and clocks under glass domes—of the farmhouse that contained the Officers' Mess. Outside, a widespread uproar was distantly audible : shouts, the revving of jeep and motor-cycle engines, the braying of a trombone that was being blown through rather than played. Ten minutes ago what sounded very much like a long burst of light-machine-gun fire had come from the direction of the Signal Office. There was no reason to suppose that all this was a demonstration of Socialist triumph over cowed and silent Tories. Whether or not Doll was right about the motives which had prompted the return of a Labour Government in Great Britain, the local reaction to it tonight was largely non-political in temper.

"They're keeping hard at it," Doll said, pointing out of the open window to a sudden burst of flame somewhere across the road. It was brighter than the now hour-old bonfire in the billet area. A few figures could be seen in the light of the new conflagration, reeling in and out of the darkness like pantomime drunks. "Funny how nobody seems to be interfering. The major's right about one thing, anyway. Discipline's going. Ah, thank you, sir." He raised one of the glasses of whisky which the Mess corporal had brought in response to Archer's bellow. "Well. A solemn moment. What shall it be ? I give you England, Mr. Archer."

"England." Not your England, Archer said to himself, not the petrol-flogging C.Q.M.S.'s England, not the major's England or Cleaver's England or the Adjutant's or the Colonel's or Jack Rowney's or Tom Thurston's England, but to a certain extent Hargreaves's England and absolutely my England, full of girls and drinks and jazz and books and decent houses and decent jobs and being your own boss. He said in a friendly tone : "I wonder whether England's going to turn out the way you'd like her to."

"Oh, I've no doubt she won't, sir. But that's not really going to concern me much. I shan't be there, you see. Emigration's the thing for me, as soon as I can fix it up."

"Really? Where are you thinking of? Canada? Australia?"

"I think Africa, Mr. Archer. A place where there's room for initiative and where a determined man can still make his way. Kenya, perhaps, or one of the Rhodesias. There's some scope there. No, I've been thinking about it for a long time and today's news really decided me. Taken a load off my mind, in a way. Funny thing, I should be feeling depressed, with the Socialists getting in, but I don't at all. Quite the contrary, in fact." Doll drained his glass.

"How about another of those?"

"No, thank you, sir, I really should be getting along and seeing the major. It's what I came for, after all."

"I'll take you up."

"There is just one point you might be able to help me with first, sir, if you would." Doll opened the buff file-cover he had brought with him. "This posting advice. I expect you know how the major's got all that organised. He can send who he likes. Well, he's asked to provide eight bodies of various kinds. All signal-office personnel. They'll be entraining for the U.K. in a couple of days, twenty-eight days' leave, then the boat for Burma. I should imagine they'll all be joining the same unit out there. Now the major's been in a funny mood recently. Sort of withdrawn. Normally he'd nominate all these bodies personally, but this morning he

gave me three names and told me to fill in the others myself. Not like him at all. Anyway, I was just wondering if
there's anybody in your section you'd care to lose. Apart
from Hargreaves, that is. He was one of the major's three,
as you probably know."

"Yes, he did mention it to me. Tell me, Sergeant Doll, is
there a vacancy for a switchboard-operator on that list?"

"There is, sir. Two, in fact."

"Mm. It's tempting, but I'm afraid———"

"Perhaps it'll help you to make up your mind, Mr.
Archer, if I tell you now that I wasn't going to bother the
major with signing the order himself. He's got enough on
his mind already. And of course any officer's signature
would do. Yours, for instance, sir."

Archer hesitated. "He's bound to see the file copy."

"Yes, sir, but that won't be until tomorrow morning, will
it? And I was thinking of dropping the top copy off for
transmission at the Signal Office tonight when I go back
down. Get it out of the way."

"He could cancel it and send an amended list."

"Oh, do you think that's likely, sir? Major Raleigh wants
to be thought of as someone who can take a quick decision
and stick to it. It's like a moral code with him."

"A good point, Sergeant. Very well, then. I think I'll
nominate Signalman Hammond."

"14156755 Signalman Hammond, J. R., S.B.O. D.II?"
Doll ran his fingertip along a line of typing. "Anybody else?
Right. Now, if you'd just sign here, sir.... Thank you. I
suppose you'll be off yourself soon, Mr. Archer, won't you,
after what you were telling me?"

"I imagine so. Well, you won't be needing the major
after all now, I suppose."

"Oh yes I will, sir. That was just a routine matter. Something far more important has come up. There's a signal here from War Office telling 424 Wireless Section, 502 Line Section and 287 D.R. Section to stand by to move on twenty-four hours' notice. Half the Company. They've obviously decided we're to be broken up."

"That's important all right," Archer said. "To the major more than anyone else, probably."

"My feeling exactly, sir. That was why I thought it couldn't wait till the morning. I reckoned I had to let him know about it tonight." Doll's eyes grew distant.

"He'd set his heart on taking the Company out East."

"Oh, don't I know it, Mr. Archer. That's the end of that ambition. I wonder what the next pipe-dream will be." Suddenly getting to his feet, Doll roamed about the room with his hands in his pockets, an uncharacteristic bodily movement. "It may surprise you to learn, sir," he said cordially, "that I'm by way of being a bit of an angler. Been at it since I was a boy. Well now, it used to surprise me very much at first how badly I got on with other anglers. Jealousy rather than congratulations if you managed to pull off something a bit out of the ordinary. No end of disagreements over red hackles and what-not. And a lot of boredom too. Now in one way you wouldn't expect that, sir, would you? You'd expect people who'd got interests in common to get on better with one another than the average, not worse. But when you come to think about it it's not so odd. Someone who's a bit like yourself can rub you up the wrong way worse than a chap who's totally different. Well, there's one obvious instance. I bet a lot of the lads in this Company hate their officers and N.C.O.s a sight worse than they ever hated Jerry. They know them, you see.

"You'll have to forgive me for reciting you a sermon, Mr. Archer, but this is a point about human nature that's always interested me. And it has got an application. I take it I wouldn't be intruding on your mental privacy, so to speak, sir, if I hazarded a guess that you regard myself and the major as pretty much birds of a feather?"

"I think that's fair enough."

"Thank you, sir. In that case it may surprise you to learn that I can't think of anybody whom I despise as thoroughly as I despise the major. I know you hate him yourself or I wouldn't risk telling you this. You'll be leaving us soon anyway."

Archer's puzzlement, which had been growing for the last five minutes, changed direction. "But I've got personal reasons."

"I too. Though they're quite different from yours. He's so sure he's better. But in fact he's shoddy material. Third rate. Not to be depended on. In many parts of the world over the next few years an important battle's going to be fought—largely against the ideas that you yourself stand for, sir, if I may say so with all respect. The major's going to be worse than useless to us there. To me and the people who think as I do. He's soft. He'll break. I can see him standing as a Labour candidate in ten years' time if the wind's still blowing that way. No principle. That's the one thing I can't forgive."

Partly to throw off complacency at being taken into a Fascist's confidence, Archer stood up briskly and said: "I'll take you up to the major now."

"Right, sir. I wish I'd been there to see him thrown out of that last parliament. Good for Hargreaves. And you yourself too, sir, of course."

The muffled bang of an exploding petrol-tank reached them as they climbed the steep narrow stairs to the main ante-room. This had been created by the folding-back of folding doors between two former bedrooms and the importation of furniture from all over the house and elsewhere. Outside it was a tiny landing hedged by slender carved banisters. Archer left Doll here and went in.

The major was sitting in half of the curious high-backed double armchair, a favourite of his despite its clear resemblance to part of a railway-carriage seat. Probably he found it suited his characteristic activity, the having of a word, whether denunciatory or conspiratorial, with someone. He had been having one now, an earnest one accompanied by gesture, with the young and usually solitary lieutenant-colonel of Engineers whose thirst for schnapps had established him as a local personality. In his hand at the moment was a glass not of schnapps but of the Mess's whisky, a glass which, appearance suggested, had been emptied and refilled several times that evening. The colonel was rather elaborately accoutred with belt, holster, revolver and lanyard. Both he and the major, who likewise seemed to have taken drink, were dramatically illuminated by a many-tiered candelabrum that made great use of frosted glass.

Raleigh had interrupted his confidential word with the colonel to have a more public one with the Mess corporal, who was saying: "About forty, I should say, sir. Well dressed. Quite respectable."

"And where's this picture she says she wants?"

"It was in her bedroom when it was her bedroom, sir."

"But it isn't her bedroom any more. The house isn't hers either, it's been requisitioned. It belongs to me. No, she can't have her picture. I don't care whether she painted it herself or not, she can't have it. Go and tell her so, will you?"

When he saw that Archer was near, the major turned his back as far as was possible without actually kneeling on his seat. The emotion he felt for the ex-Speaker of the now officially dissolved parliament was not military disapprobation nor yet personal anger, but sadness at the other's withholding of loyalty. All this and much more had been gone into at length the morning after Hargreaves had spied strangers. Archer had protested, with every appearance of sincerity, that the strangers could have been suffered to remain if anybody had thought to put forward a simple motion proposing this, and that nothing but general ignorance of procedure had brought about their exit. Raleigh paid no heed. In the course of a sad and objective appraisal of Archer's disloyalty he had recounted rumours about Archer's private life which, if repeated before witnesses and if the law of slander had run in the Army, might have been the occasion of awards in damages sufficient to buy and sell the contents of the Officers' Shop. Then, still avowing sadness, the major had announced that his duty to the Company forbade the retention in its ranks of anybody so provenly disloyal. In other words, it was Burma for Archer as soon as the major's pal at H.Q. could fix it. After that, the major had sadly shouted at Archer to get out of his sight.

Archer had, and as far as possible had stayed there. But now he had to get back into it for a moment. To facilitate this he leant against the sideboard (could it have been made of ebony?) and faced the couple in the double armchair.

The R.E. colonel, whose name was Davison, was not the kind of man to appeal to Raleigh. He was what Raleigh was fond of calling a disorganised sort of chap, meaning someone whose character had not been stripped down like a racing-car until nothing but more or less military components remained. But it was his policy to encourage colonels and such to be around. Colonel Davison, once acquainted with the volume and regularity of the Mess's liquor supply, had needed no encouragement. At the moment he was saying in his public-school voice (another selling-point for the major): "But as I keep telling you, that's why the Army's so good. Because nobody could take the bloody nonsense seriously."

The major came back with something inaudible to Archer, probably that he couldn't go all the way with the colonel there.

"Well, nobody with any sense, then," Davison said. "And that saves an awful lot of worry. Means you can start laughing."

Again the major could not be heard, but this time he went on much longer. Davison listened, nodding steadily, his eyes on his glass, which he was rotating on the knee of his crossed leg. Archer's attention wandered. It came to rest on Cleaver, who was half-lying on a purple sofa reading an unexpurgated edition of *Lady Chatterley's Lover*. Archer had had a go at that too. General opinion in the Mess was that it ranked about halfway in the little library the batmen had been assiduously building up ever since the Company entered urban France: not so good as, say, Frank Harris's *My Life and Loves,* but clearly better than the available non-fictional treatments of these themes, vital books by Scotsmen with titles like *Married Happiness.* Cleaver laughed silently to himself, then looked quickly and furtively round without catching Archer's eye.

"It's all a joke," Davison said loudly. "The whole thing."

The major saw Archer. "Yes?"

"Sergeant Doll would like to see you, sir. He's just outside."

When Raleigh had gone, Davison patted the space beside him. "Come and sit down, laddie."

"Thank you, sir."

"Sir. Sir sir sir. Sir sir sir sir sir sir sir. Ha."

From the way Davison swayed about in his seat as he said this, Archer concluded that he was not just drunk, but very drunk. "Nice little place we've got here, don't you think?"

"Oh, delightful. Delightful. Your poor major's upset. Have you been being nasty to him? Have a drink. Corporal! More whisky needed here. Crash priority."

"I'm never nasty to majors," Archer said.

"Aren't you? I am. All the time. One of the consummations. Compensations. What do you do in Civvy Street, laddie?" The colonel was perhaps five years older than Archer.

"I don't do anything. Not yet. I was a student."

"Jolly good luck to you. I'm an electrical engineer. So of course they put me on bridges. But it's all experience. A very good preparation, the Army."

"For what?"

"Everything."

As they received their drinks, Archer became aware that an altercation was going on just outside the room, with raised voices and what sounded like part of a human frame bouncing off the door. Was Doll fighting Raleigh?

"Just about everything. You'll have learnt a lot in the

last few years which will stand you in good stead when you get into the great world."

Archer's mouth opened. "You mean that this is what *life* is like?"

"Roughly."

Doll called from the doorway. "Would you come, **Mr.** Archer, quickly?"

Archer hurried over, followed by Davison, who said : "If there's anything to see I'm going to see it."

Four men confronted one another in the confined space at the stairhead : Hargreaves, Sergeant Fleming, Doll and Raleigh. Whatever he might have been doing a moment earlier, Hargreaves was doing nothing now except being held from behind by Fleming and denounced by Raleigh. Doll stood to one side, his file under his arm.

"I didn't know anything like this was going to happen, sir," Fleming shouted to Archer. "He just said very quiet he'd like to see the major if he was free, to apologise to him about the parliament, and I said couldn't it wait till the morning, and he said, still very quiet, his conscience was——"

"You dare come here and say that to me," Raleigh shouted through this. His soft face had a glistening flush. "You dirty little homo. Can't leave a decent lad alone. Rotten to the core. I know what goes on in that billet of yours. I'm going to take you off that draft and have you court-martialled for . . . for filth. There are plenty of people who'd be only too glad——"

Cleaver stepped forward and caught him by the arm. "Shut up, major. Pipe down, you bloody fool. Come back in here, for Christ's sake."

The major shook off Cleaver's hand. The movement

brought him face to face with Archer. A theatrical sneer twisted Raleigh's soft features. "And as for you ... Tarred with the same brush. An officer. Selected for his qualities of leadership. That's good. I like that."

There was a pause. The moment it was over Archer realised that he should have used it either to help Fleming get Hargreaves down the stairs or help Cleaver get Raleigh back into the ante-room. He could even have told the major just a little of what he thought of him. But he spent the time quailing under the major's stare.

Panting a little, Raleigh took up a fighting stance in front of Hargreaves. At the same time Colonel Davison spoke from the edge of the group. "That'll do, everybody." Fleming's expression made Archer turn quickly. He saw with incredulity that Davison was leaning against the door-jamb and levelling his drawn revolver in Raleigh's general direction.

"Often wanted to use this," Davison said. He was thin and very tall. "Properly, I mean. Not just on pigeons. Well, better late than never."

"Put that away, Colonel," Cleaver said.

Davison grinned. "Sounds as if I'm exposing myself. But I know what you mean. My turn now. Who's gonna make me?"

"Let's be sensible."

At this, Davison collapsed in laughter. "One up to you, by God. Funny, isn't it?—always turns out like this if you try to do anything. Chaps saying let's be sensible. Let's be that whatever we do. Oh, my Christ."

Still laughing, he staggered through the group and ended up by the banisters, laboriously trying to fit his revolver back into its holster. The major swung back towards Hargreaves. Afterwards opinion was divided on whether he was really going to hit him, but Doll evidently thought so, for he bounded forward and shouldered the major aside. Raleigh collided hard with Davison, whose attention was distracted by his revolver and holster and who at once, with a single cracking of wood, fell through the banisters and down into the tiled hall. He landed with another cracking sound which made the backs of Archer's thighs turn cold. Doll ran down the stairs, closely followed by Cleaver. Hargreaves said: "I'm sorry, Mr. Archer."

v

"Cup of tea for you, sir. And the newspapers."

"Thank you. Did you get on to the hospital?" Major Raleigh spoke almost without inflection, as he usually did these days.

"Yes, sir. Progress maintained. Too early yet to say when he'll be up and about again, but the concussion's definitely not as bad as they thought at first and the arm's coming along as well as can be expected after a complicated fracture."

Outside, heavy transport could be heard toiling in low gear. "What's that row?"

"That's 424 Wireless forming up to move out, sir. They're due at the railhead at fifteen hundred hours."

"I know."

"Are you going down to see them off, sir?"

"No."

"Oh, by the way, Colonel Davison sent you a message, sir."

"Did he?"

"Yes, he did, sir. Thanks for the party and he hopes he wasn't a nuisance."

The major screwed up his soft face as a motor-bike revved up in the road below. "Shut the window, will you, Doll?"

"Right, sir." The operation completed, Doll turned round and leant against the sill. "Well, we've all been very lucky, sir, really, haven't we? Things might have turned out much more serious. By the way, I thought you were very wise not to go on with that idea of yours of having Hargreaves court-martialled. Very wise indeed, sir."

"When I want your opinion of my decisions, Doll, I'll ask for it." This tripped less well off the major's tongue than it might have done at another time. Only Colonel Davison's accident had prevented that last encounter with Hargreaves from degenerating into a serious breach of order. The persistence of this thought bothered Raleigh. He said wearily: "And while you're here I'd like you to tell me in detail how Hammond got on to that list with Hargreaves."

"I've nothing to add to my previous account, sir, but still. You asked me to complete the list at my discretion, right? So seeing Hargreaves's name there, and knowing that Hammond was his mate, I put him down too. We've always done that sort of thing."

"Is that all you knew?"

"Why, of course, sir. What else is there to know?"

"How did Archer come to sign that message?"

"Well, again as before, sir, Mr. Archer happened to call in at the Orderly Room and I asked him, as I might have asked any officer who was available. There were one or two things piled up and I wanted to get them off."

"Did Mr. Archer read it through before he signed it?"

"I really couldn't say, sir. Quite likely he had enough confidence in me not to bother. You've often done the same yourself, sir, and believe me I very much appreciate the implied compliment."

"Are you telling me the truth, Doll?"

"Mr. Archer will confirm every word I've said, sir, as far as it concerns him."

The major sighed heavily. "I suppose that's that."

"I suppose so, sir. Actually it's a pity we've lost Hammond, a very pleasant young fellow I agree, but it's not going to make much difference, sir, is it? There'd have been nothing for him to do here after the Signal Office closes down next week. I don't suppose any of us will be together much longer. Captain Cleaver and Mr. Archer and the others on twenty-four-hour warning. You'll be all on your own here before very long, sir."

"I'm looking forward to it."

Doll almost smiled. "Of course, it's Mr. Archer who's come best out of this. Dodging the Far East after all. What a bit of luck that was, eh, sir?"

Something close to attention entered the major's manner. "Dodging the Far East?"

"Oh, no doubt about it, sir. Even if he goes tomorrow it'll take him ten days to get home, the way things are. Then he'll go on twenty-eight days' leave, which'll bring him to the first week in September. And with his release due a month at most after that it wouldn't be worth anybody's while to put him on a boat. No, he's——"

"Doll, I don't know what you're talking about."

"Really, sir? I'm awfully sorry, I was sure Mr. Archer would have told you long ago. When was he telling me about it, now? Yes, I can remember exactly—it was the earlier part of the evening on which Colonel Davison met with his accident. Mr. Archer and I went on to discuss the Election results—that's right—and then we——"

"All right, I don't want the story of your life. I asked you to tell me——"

"Do forgive me, sir—I've got this bad habit of letting my tongue run away with me, I know. It's just that the events of that evening are so indelibly impressed on my memory, sir, if you know what I—Yes, sir. Well, Mr. Archer showed me a letter from the head of his college in Oxford, the Master I think he called himself. It said they were arranging his release from the Army and reckoned he'd be out in good time to go into the college when the term begins, which I gather is about the 10th of October, though no doubt you could put me right there."

"But he's only been in for three or four years. You and I and most of the blokes have been in for six."

"Seven in my case, sir; you'll recall that I was one of the 1938 militiamen. Yes, I know it seems strange, Mr. Archer getting out so soon, but apparently this is something called the Class 'B' Scheme—we had a memo about it a couple of weeks ago which I'll look out for you if you're interested."

"Don't bother."

"How funny Mr. Archer hasn't told you yet. I expect he's waiting for a suitable opportunity, sir, don't you?"

"Get out and leave me in peace."

"Glad to, sir."

Left in peace, the major sat on at his almost-empty table. The bulk of 424 Wireless Section was evidently moving out on to the main road along Raleigh's Alley, making full use of that thoroughfare for the first and last time. The major's eye missed a letter from the British Drama League saying that *Journey's End* was not available. It caught an order informing him that with effect from two days' time the area of which he had hoped to become chieftain would be known as No. 9 Independent Transit Area and would fall under the command of a full colonel despatched from H.Q. He picked up a newspaper headlined *IT'S NO JOKE-IO TO LIVE IN TOKYO: 600 Super-Forts Blast Jap Heartland* and put it down again. The other paper contained a large Election supplement. He summoned the resolution to study the details of what he had so far been able to take in only as an appalling generality. Turning to an inner page, he read:

WINKWORTH (WEST)

R. Jack (Lab.)	28,740
Maj.-Gen. P. O. de C. Biggs-Courtenay, D.S.O. (C.)	9,011
Lab. majority	19,729

LABOUR GAIN FROM CONSERVATIVE

1935: Maj.-Gen. P. O. de C. Biggs-Courtenay, D.S.O. (C.) 19,495; W. Mott (Lab.) 9,319: C. majority 10,176

The major dropped his head into his hands. This, he supposed, was the bottom. And yet he felt a stirring of hope. Having sunk to the lowest depths his nature was capable of, he could not help seeing the future as some sort of upward path. Nobody and nothing in his immediate environment gave him the smallest reason for confidence. Doll, Cleaver, Hammond, Davison, Archer (whom he had tried so hard to train up as a conscientious officer), the Company, the Signal Office, chances of leadership—all in their different ways had turned out to be not worth depending on. But the world was wide. Bad things could happen and it all went on as before. The thought of his friends in Potsdam filled him with encouragement now, not envy. Much of what he believed in must survive.

And the guarantee of that was England. England had been up against it in 1940, in 1914 and no doubt earlier, with the Napoleon business and so on. She had weathered every storm, she had never gone under. All that was needed was faith. Despite everything that Hargreaves and Archer and the rest of them might do, England would muddle through somehow.

MORAL FIBRE

MORAL FIBRE

"Hallo," I said. "Who are you?" I said it to a child of about three who was pottering about on the half landing between the ground floor of the house, where some people called Davies lived, and the first floor, where I and my wife and children lived. The child now before me was not one of mine. He looked old-fashioned in some way, probably because instead of ordinary children's clothes he wore scaled-down versions of grown-up clothes, including miniature black lace-up boots. His eyes were alarmed or vacant, their roundness repeated in the rim of the amber-coloured dummy he was sucking. As I approached he ran incompetently away up the further flight. I'd tried to speak heartily to him, but most likely had only sounded accusing. Accusing was how I often felt in those days, especially after a morning duty in the Library Reference Room, being talked to most of the way by my colleague, Ieuan Jenkins, and about his wife's headaches too.

I mounted in my turn and entered the kitchen, where my own wife, called Jean, was straining some potatoes into the wash-hand basin that did, but only just did, as a sink. "Hallo, darling," she said. "How were the borrowers this morning, then?"

"They were readers this morning, not borrowers," I said, kissing her.

"Aw, same thing."

"Yes, that's right. They were as usual, I'm sorry to say. Who was that extraordinary child I saw on the stairs?"

"Ssshh. . . . Must have been one of Betty's. She had to bring them with her." Jean pointed towards the sitting-room, where clicks and thumps suggesting domestic work could be heard.

"Betty's?" I whispered. "What's going on?"

"She's just finishing up in there. Betty Arnulfsen. You remember, the girl Mair Webster was going to fix us up with. You know."

"Oh, the delinquent. I'd forgotten all about it."

"She's coming to lunch."

"Betty Arnulfsen?"

"No, Mair, dull."

"Oh, Christ."

"Now, don't be nasty, John. She's been very kind to us. Just because she's a bit boring, that doesn't mean she . . ."

"*Just* because. A *bit* boring. If it were only that. The woman's a menace, a threat to Western values. Terrifying to think of her being a social worker. All that awful know-ing-best stuff, being quite sure what's good for people and not standing any nonsense and making them knuckle under and going round saying how she fully appreciates the seri-ousness and importance of her job, as if that made it all all right. They bloody well ought to come and ask me before they let anybody be a social worker."

"Then there wouldn't be any. You can take these plates in. She'll be here any minute."

It was all most interesting, and in a way that things that

happened to me hardly ever were. Mair Webster, who knew us because her husband was a senior colleague of mine on the staff of the Aberdarcy (Central) Public Library, had brought off what must have seemed to her a smart double coup by providing, as the twice-a-week domestic help we craved, one of the fallen women with whom her municipal duties brought her into contact. It had turned out that the woman in question wasn't really fallen, just rather inadmissibly inclined from the perpendicular. She'd had an illegitimate child or two and had recently or some time ago neglected or abandoned it or them—Mair had a gift of unmemorability normally reserved for far less emphatic characters—but that was all over now and the girl was taking proper care of her young, encouraged by her newly acquired husband, a Norwegian merchant seaman and a "pretty good type" according to Mair, who went on about it as if she'd masterminded the whole thing. Perhaps she had. Anyway, meeting Betty Arnulfsen was bound to be edifying, however imperfectly fallen she might be.

In the sitting-room, which doubled as dining-room and lunching-room when people like Mair were about, a smallish dark girl of nineteen or twenty was rearranging rugs and pushing chairs back into position. At my entry the child I'd seen earlier tottered behind the tall boxlike couch, where another of the same size was already lurking. Of this supplementary child I could make out nothing for certain, apart from a frizzy but sparse head of ginger hair. The girl had looked up at me and then quickly and shyly away again.

"Good morning," I said, in the sort of tone officials visiting things are fond of and good at. I seemed not to have chosen this tone. It wasn't my day for tones.

"Morning, Mr. Lewis," she muttered, going on with her work.

"Miserable old weather."

This notification, although accurate enough as far as it went, drew no reply. I fussed round the gate-leg table for a bit, fiddling with plates and cutlery and stealthily watching Betty Arnulfsen. Her straight black hair was ribboned in place by what looked like the belt of an old floral-pattern dress. In her plain skirt and jumper and with her meek expression she had the air of an underpaid shopgirl or bullied supply teacher. She wore no make-up. Altogether she wasn't my idea of a delinquent, but then few people are my idea of anything.

There was a ring at the front-door bell, a favourite barking-trigger of the dog that lived downstairs. On my wife's orders I went and let in Mair Webster, whose speed off the verbal mark proved to be at its famed best. By the time we reached the kitchen I already had a sound general grasp of the events of her morning. These included a bawling out of the Assistant Child Care Officer down at the Town Hall and a longer, fiercer, more categorical bawling out of the foster-mother of one of "her" babies. "Is Betty here?" she added without pause. "Hallo, Jean dear, sorry I'm late, been dreadfully pushed this morning, everybody screaming for help. How's Betty getting on? Where is she? I just want to have a word with her a minute."

I was close enough behind Mair to see the children returning to defensive positions behind the couch and Betty looking harried. It was my first view of her in full face and I thought her quite pretty, but pale and washed out. I also noticed that the ginger-haired child was sucking a dummy similar to that of its fellow.

"Ah, good morning, Betty," Mair said bluffly. "How are you getting on? Do you like working for Mrs. Lewis?"

"Aw, all right."

Mair's lion-like face took on the aspect of the king of beasts trying to outstare its tamer. "I think you know my name, don't you, Betty? It's polite to use it, you know."

At this I went out into the kitchen again, but not quickly enough to avoid hearing Betty saying, "Sorry, Mrs. Webster," and, as I shut the door behind me, Mair saying, "That's more like it, isn't it, Betty?"

"What's the matter with you?" Jean asked me.

I stopped stage-whispering obscenities and spoke some instead, using them to point or fill out a report of the recent exchange. In a moment the sitting-room door was reopened, catching me in mid-scatalogism, and Mair's voice asked my wife to come in "a minute." At the ensuing conference, I was told later, Betty's willingness, industry and general efficiency as a domestic help were probed and a favourable account of them given. Meanwhile I put to myself the question whether the removal of all social workers, preferably by execution squads, wouldn't do everyone a power of good. You had to do something about ill-treated etc. children all right, but you could see to that without behaving like a sort of revivalist military policeman.

The meeting next door broke up. Betty and her children were hurried out of the place, the former carrying a tattered parcel my wife had furtively thrust into her hands. I found out afterwards that among other things it contained a tweed skirt of Jean's I particularly liked her in and my own favourite socks. This was charity run riot.

At lunch, Mair said efficiently: "The trouble with girls like that is that they've got no moral fibre."

"How do you mean?" I asked.

"I mean this, John. They've no will of their own, you see. They just drift. Line of least resistance all the time. Now Betty didn't really want to abandon those twins of hers— she was quite a good mother to them, apparently, when she was living with her parents and going out to work at this café. Then she went to a dance and met this dirty swine of a crane driver and he persuaded her to go and live with him—he's got a wife and child himself, a real beauty, he is —and he wouldn't take the twins, so she just went off and left them and let her parents look after them. Then the swine went off with another woman and Betty's father wouldn't have her back in the house. Said he'd forgiven her once when she had the twins when she was sixteen and he wasn't going to forgive her again. He's strong chapel, you see, believes in sinners being cast into the outer darkness, you know the kind of thing. It's a tragic story, isn't it?"

"Yes," I said, and went on to talk about the conflict between generations, I think it was. Mair's technique when others ventured beyond a couple of sentences was to start nodding, stepping up the tempo as long as they continued. When her face was practically juddering with nods I gave in.

"Well," she went on in a satisfied tone, "going back to where I was just now, Betty's father got into such a rage with her that he threw the twins out as well, and she got her job back at the café, which wasn't really a good thing because it's not a very desirable place, but at least it meant that there was some money coming in, but she couldn't take the twins to work with her, so she parked them with the woman she was renting her room from. Then she, the woman, went out for the evening one time when she was

working late, Betty I mean, and the twins were left un-
attended and they ran out into the street and wandered
about and a policeman found them and that's how we got
brought into it. They were in a dreadful state, poor little
dabs, half in rags and—quite filthy. I had the devil's own
job stopping them being taken into care, I can tell you. You
see, while Betty was with her parents in a decent home she
looked after them all right, but on her own, with bad
examples all round her, she just let things slide. No moral
fibre there, I'm afraid. Well, I fixed her up at the day
nursery—didn't know there were such things, she said, but
I told her she'd just been too lazy to inquire—and after that
things jogged along until this Norwegian came into the café
for a cup of tea and saw Betty and bob's your uncle."

"Hasn't the Norwegian got to go back to Norway ever?"
Jean asked, her eyes on the forkful of fish that had been
oscillating for some minutes between Mair's plate and her
mouth.

"He's going over for a few weeks soon, he says. He's got
a job at a chandler's in Ogmore Street—it's run by Nor-
wegians, like a lot of them. Decent people. They've been
married six weeks now, him and Betty, and he's very fond
of the twins and keeps her up to the mark about them, and
of course I give her a good pep talk every so often."

"Of course," I said.

"One job I had to do was take her out of that café. Lot
of undesirables hang round the place, you know. A girl like
Betty, quite pretty and none too bright, she'd have been just
their meat. It's something to have kept her out of their
clutches. Oh, yes, I'm quite proud of myself in a way."

One Sunday afternoon a couple of months later I was

dozing in front of the fire—Jean had taken the kids out for a walk with a pal of hers and the pal's kids—when the doorbell rang. Wondering if the caller mightn't at last be some beautiful borrower come to avow her love, I hurried downstairs. The person on the doorstep was certainly a woman and probably on the right side of thirty, but she wasn't beautiful. Nor—I'd have taken any odds—was she a borrower, not with that transparent mac, that vehement eye shadow, that squall of scent. "Good afternoon," I said.

The woman smiled, fluttering her Prussian-blue eyelids. "You remember me, don't you, Mr. Lewis? Betty Arnulfsen."

I felt my own eyes dilate. "Why, of course," I said genially. "How are you, Betty? Do come in."

"Aw, all right, thank you. Thanks."

"Haven't seen you for a long time." Not for several weeks, in fact. She'd turned up three more times to do our chores and then that had suddenly been that. Application to Mair Webster had produced an evasive answer—an extreme and, as I now saw it, suspicious rarity.

"I was just passing by, see, so I thought I'd drop in and see how you was all getting along, like."

"Good. It's very nice to see you again. Well, what have you been doing with yourself?"

It could have been more delicately put, for somebody, whether herself or not, had plainly been doing a good deal with Betty one way and another. As we stood confronted by the sitting-room fire I saw that her hair, which had been of a squaw-like sleekness, now looked like some kind of petrified black froth, and that her face was puffy underneath the yellowish coating of make-up. At the same time she'd altogether lost her hounded look : she seemed sure of

herself, even full of fun. She wore a tight lilac costume with
purple stripes on it and carried a long-handled umbrella
that had elaborate designs on the plastic.

"Aw, I been doing lots of things," she said in answer to
my question. "Having a bit of a good time for a change.
Soon got brassed off with that old cow Webster telling me
what I must do and what I mustn't do. I been keeping out
of her way, going to live my own life for a change, see? I
got a bit of money now. Here, have a fag."

"No, thanks, I don't smoke."

"Go on, it'll do you good, man."

"No, honestly, I never do."

"I can tell you're one of the careful ones." She laughed
quite a bit at this stroke, giving me a chance to notice the
purplish inner portions of her lips where the lipstick had
worn away or not reached. With a kind of indulgent contempt, she went on: "And how you been keeping? Still
working down that old library?"

"Oh, yes, I feel I ought to give them a hand occasionally."

"Don't you get brassed off with it now and then?"

"Yes, I do, but I keep going. Can't afford to weaken."

"That's the boy. Got to keep the dough coming in,
haven't you?"

"Well, it helps, you know."

"What you pulling in down there? Never mind, don't
suppose you want to say. What you get up to after work?"

"Nothing out of the ordinary."

"What you do, then, when you goes out for a night?
Where do you go?"

"Oh, just here and there. I sometimes have a few along
at the corner, at the General Picton."

"I expect you got your own mates." Her cigarette had gone out and she relit it. She wasn't really at home with it: smoking was something she was still in the process of taking up. After spitting out a shred of tobacco, she said: "Never go round the pubs in Ogmore Street, do you?"

"Not as a rule, no."

(Ogmore Street leads into the docks, and on these and associated grounds is usually steered well clear of during the hours of darkness by persons of refinement and discrimination.)

"We gets up to some games down Ogmore Street. We haves the time of our bloody lives, we do."

"I bet you do."

"Yeah," she said with great conviction. "Jean gone out, have she?"

"Just taken the kids for a breath of fresh air. I don't suppose she'll be long."

"Ah. They all right, the kids?"

"Pretty fair. What are you up to yourself these days?"

She gave a great yell of laughter. "That's a question, that is. What don't I bloody get up to? What am I up to, eh? That's a good one." Then her manner grew seriously informative. "I got in with the business girls now, see?"

"Oh, really?" A momentary vision of Betty drinking morning coffee at the Kardomah with a group of secretaries and shorthand typists was briefly presented to me, before being penetrated by her true meaning. "Er . . . good fun?"

"It's all right, you know. Got its points, like. See what I got here." She opened her handbag, a shiny plastic affair in a pink pastel shade, and, after I'd sat there wondering for a moment or two, drew out a roll of crumpled pound notes

bound with an elastic band. "Take you a long time to pull
in this much down the library, wouldn't it?"

"Oh, no doubt about that."

"We goes with the boys round the docks and the sailors
when they comes off the ships. They're the best. They wants
a bit of fun and they don't care what they pays for it. They
got plenty of dough, see? They goes on the bloody binge
down there. Lots of Norgies we gets. I like the Norgies."

"Oh, yes, your husband's one, isn't he?"

This second deviation from the path of true tact was as
little heeded as the first. "That's right. He've gone back to
Norway now."

"For good?"

"No, don't think so. Father in trouble or something.
Reckon he'll fetch up again some time."

"How are the twins?" The domestic note, once struck,
might be a handy one to prolong. What was the time?
Where was Jean? Would she bring her red-faced English
oh-I-say-darling pal back with her? Why not?

"They're okay. I got someone looking after them okay.
These Norgies are dead funny, though. Makes me die. The
Welsh boys, now, they likes me with my vest on, don't want
it no other way, but the Norgies don't care for that, they
wants everything off, and they don't like it outside, they
always goes home with you for it. They likes to take their
time, like. You know Joe Leyshon?"

"I've heard of him. Used to be in the fight game, didn't
he?"

"He runs a lot of the girls down Ogmore Street, but I
won't let him run me. He wants to run me, but I don't like
him. Some of his mates is dead funny, though. We broke
into a shop the other night over Cwmharan way. Didn't get

anything much, few fags and things, but we had a laugh. Mad buggers, they are. We goes down the Albany mostly. You know the Albany? It's all right. You ought to come down there one night and have a couple of drinks and a bit of fun. What about it? I'm going down there tonight."

"Well, I don't want to come barging in...."

"Go on, I'd show you around, you wouldn't come to no harm, I promise you. They're all right there, really. I'd see you had a good time. You could tell Jean you was out with your mates, see?"

"It's very kind of you, Betty, but honestly I don't think I could. I'm pretty well fixed up here, you know what I mean, and so I don't..."

"I tell you one thing, John."

"What's that?"

"You're afraid to go with me."

So many factors amalgamated to put this beyond serious dispute that reply was difficult. "Oh, I wouldn't say that," I said after a moment, trying to ram jocoseness into tone and manner. "No, I wouldn't say that at all."

Betty evidently saw through this. She said: "You are. You're afraid."

"It isn't that exactly. It's just that I try to stick to my wife as far as possible," I told her, certain that I sounded like some ferret-faced Christian lance-corporal in a barrack-room discussion.

"Yeah, I know, you'd fold up if you hadn't got her to cling on to. You hangs around all the bloody time." Contempt had returned to her voice, edged this time with bitterness, but she showed none of either when she went on to add: "You're a good boy."

"I wouldn't say—I don't know. Betty, you mustn't mind me saying this, but isn't it rather risky to go round breaking into places with these pals of yours? Aren't you afraid of getting caught?"

"Aw, short life and a merry one's what I say. It's worth it for a bit of excitement. Don't get much chance of a thrill these days, eh?"

"Well, it's up to you, but you don't want to get—you know—sent down, do you? The twins wouldn't have . . ."

"Don't preach, now. I gets brassed off with bloody preaching."

"I'm sorry, I didn't mean to sound like that."

"Okay." She smiled.

In the succeeding silence a door boomed shut below. The slapping gait of my daughter Eira became audible, overlaid and in part obscured by the characteristic bellowing squeal of her younger brother. Both sounds began to ascend the stairs.

"Jean back, eh?" Betty got to her feet. "I better be going."

"Oh, don't go, stay and have a cup of tea with us."

"I better not."

Eira ran into the room, stopping short when she saw Betty and then moving towards the fire by a circuitous route, hugging the wall and the couch. "Put my coat off," she said to me distantly.

"Hallo," Betty said with an elaborate rising inflection. "Hallo. And whose little girl are you? Let auntie take your coat off, then. Come on, flower. That's right. Had a lovely run, have you? Did you see any bunnies? How you've grown. And you're bold as ever, I declare. Yes, you are.

You're bold, very very bold. Yes, you are. You're very very brazen by there."

Jean came in with the baby. "Well, hallo, Betty," she said, grinning. "Nice to see you. Christ, shut up, can't you?" This last was addressed to the baby, who seemed almost, but not quite, worn out with mortal pain.

"Sorry I couldn't come along that Tuesday like we said, Mrs. Lewis, but the twins was poorly and I couldn't fix it to let you know."

"That's all right, Betty. I'll put the kettle on."

"Let me take the baby for you."

"Oh, thanks a lot. John, you might have kept the fire up."

"Sorry, dear." I picked up the coal scuttle, which was one of the obliquely-truncated-cone type. It proved to weigh less than it should, less than a coal scuttle with any coal in it could. I could hardly remember ever having made up the fire without encountering, at the very outset, a light coal scuttle.

During a long, foul-mouthed ardour in the coal cupboard under the stairs, I thought first how funny it was that a fallen woman—really fallen now, right smack over full length—should talk to a child in just the same style as the perpendicularly upright went in for. But then presumably there were parts of the fallen that were bound to remain unfallen, quite important parts too. This brought up the whole mystery of prostituted existence: not what happened to your womanhood or your springs of emotion or your chances of getting clued up on the splendours and miseries of the flesh—screw all that—but what it was like to be a prostitute during the times when you weren't actually behaving like one, when you were in mufti: on a bus, cooking the baked

beans, doing the ironing, going shopping, chatting to a
neighbour, buying the Christmas presents. It must be like
going round ordinarily and all the time you were a spy or
a parson or a leading authority on Rilke, things which you
surely often forgot about being. Anyway, to judge by the
representative upstairs, being a prostitute was something
you could be done a power of good by, and without having
to be horrible first, either. As regards not having to get horrible later on, that too could no doubt be arranged, especially if you could keep out of the way of the various sets of
men in white coats who, according to report, tended to close
in on you after a few years in the game. That was a nasty
prospect all right, and resembled many a kindred nastiness
thought up by the Godhead in seeming a disproportionate
penalty for rather obscure offences. Still, that minor cavil
about the grand design had been answered long ago, hadn't
it? Yes, more answers than one had been offered.

A little coal, too little to be worth expelling, had entered
my shoe. I bore the scuttle upstairs to find Jean and Eira in
the kitchen and Betty still holding the baby. Her demeanour
had quietened and she was more like the Betty I had first
met when she said: "You won't tell Jean all what I been
saying, will you?"

"Of course I won't."

"And you won't tell that old Webster I been up?"

"Christ, no. What do you think I am?"

"She's a cow."

"Oh, she's a cow all right."

Betty nodded slowly, frowning, half-heartedly jogging the
baby on her knee. Then she said: "She's a real cow."

This refinement upon the original concept made me
laugh. Betty joined in. We laughed together for some time,

so that Eira came in from the kitchen to see what the joke was.

"I don't mind telling you I was very depressed about that girl at one time," Mair Webster said. "Quite frankly I thought we might be going to lose her. It upset me a good deal, one way and another. Once her husband was out of the way for a couple of months, as soon as his back was turned she just took the line of least resistance. Her old cronies at the café, you see, she took up with them again, and got things fixed up with another of them there with minding each other's children while the other one was off after the men, turn and turn about and sharing the same flat, or couple of rooms rather, the most sordid den you could possibly imagine, I'm not exaggerating, I promise you. Well, I soon got Betty and the twins out of that hell hole and fixed them up in a decent place, good enough for the time being, anyway, until Arnulfsen got back from Norway. They've quite a nice little flat now—well, you'll be able to judge, John. It's nothing very grand, of course, but it's a darned sight better than what people like that are used to. Oh, thank you, Jean dear."

"Everything looks pretty bright then, doesn't it?" my wife asked, pouring coffee. "Troubles seem to be over." Her manner showed a relief that I guessed to be partly personal. The strain of not telling Mair about Betty's earlier visit hadn't been lightly borne.

"I don't think I should say that exactly," Mair said. "Arnulfsen's forgiven her all right, and she's trying to make a go of it, quite seriously, I can tell. But they keep being bothered by the crowd she used to be in with before, girls who used to be in the same gang looking her up, and once they even had a lascar trying to force his way in; wanted to renew old acquaintance and got her address from the café, I suppose. There've been one or two things like that. And then some of the neighbours have got to hear about Betty's past and they keep teasing her about it, call out in the street after her. Chapel spirit gone sour, you see. It makes Arnulfsen pretty wild."

While Jean expressed her indignation, I was wondering fairly hard how I was going to "be able to judge" the Arnulfsens' flat. Was I in some way committed to a tea party there, or what? An answer couldn't be long delayed, for Mair was draining her cup and rising. "Come along," she said to me. "We've not got too much time."

"Time for what, Mair? I'm sorry..."

She threw me a momentary leonine glare before dipping to pick up her handbag. When she spoke, it was with an incredulity to which those accustomed to plan for others must often be subject. Since what she had lined up for me was necessitated both by logic and by natural law, how could I conceivably not know what it was? "But surely you're coming along to Betty's with me? I'm only popping in to see how she is. Then I can drop you at the library by two-fifteen. Cheerio, Jean dear. Thank you for a lovely lunch. We must fix up a coffee date for next week. I'll give John a ring, if I can manage to pick a time when he's at the seat of custom."

Wiggling her eyebrows at me to enjoin silence, Jean went into a vivacious speech which lasted more or less until I was sitting in Mair's car next to its owner. Opened envelopes, typed lists, printed forms lay about us as at some perfunctory demonstration of bureaucracy at work. Jean continued her facial ballet until we left.

I knew Mair was going to tell me some more, or possibly run over a few familiar but essential points, about what being a social worker was like. She enjoyed getting me on my own and doing this because, it appeared, I was a man and, as such, easy to talk to. Sometimes her husband came into these conversations, but not often, and when he did it was likely to be as a feature of her exposition of what being married to a social worker's husband was like. I hoped we were going to get the practical today; some of Mair's case histories were of great anthropological interest, and those that weren't were still a lot better than the theoretical.

We got the theoretical, but crossed with the autobiographical, which helped a bit. What had first attracted her to the idea of social work? Ah, there were many answers to this conundrum, every one of them demanding careful or at any rate lengthy consideration. Mair had taken a course in psychology, so she knew all about the power impulse and its tendency to be present in those who made a living out of good works. Several of her colleagues were prone to this affliction, and she had even detected it in herself before now. That was where psychological training was so useful : you knew how to examine your own motives and to guard against unworthy ones. With that out of the way, she felt safe in asserting that it was the duty of the mature and responsible elements of the community to do what they could for their less gifted fellows. At one time the more conscientious kind of squire had stood in a similar relation to his tenants, the right-minded employer to his workmen and their families, but the rise of the oligopoly (Mair kept up with Labour Party research pamphlets) had put paid to all that. One of the many all-important tasks of our society was the training of specialists for functions which at one time had been discharged as by-products of other functions. A case very much in point here was provided by the constantly expanding duties of—well, Mair recognised the term *social workers*, but for her own part she preferred (having once attended a Social Science Summer School in Cardiff) to think of herself and her associates as *technicians in paternalism*.

When she brought that one out I had the infrequent experience of seeing her face express only a limited satisfaction with what she'd said. We penetrated farther into an uncongenial district. Then Mair added: "Actually, John, I'm not altogether happy about that label."

"You're not?"

"No, I'm not. It's a scientific term, of course, and so it's quite accurate in a way, but like all scientific terms it's incomplete, it doesn't really say enough, doesn't go far enough, leaves out a lot. It leaves out the thing that keeps us all going, sees us over the rough patches and stops us losing faith, which is the one thing we can't afford to do in our job. It's—well, I can't think of any better name for it than ... idealism. You can laugh if you like—" she turned her profile far enough round to assure me that any such laughter had better remain internal—"but that's what it is. Just a simple, old-fashioned urge to do good, not in a chapel way, naturally, but scientifically, because we know what we're doing, but that's the basis of the whole thing, no point in beating about the bush. I know that sort of talk makes you feel uncomfortable, but I believe in——"

Before she could mention calling a spade a spade, a mode of nomenclature she often recommended, I told her that that wasn't quite it, and went on: "This isn't aimed at you, Mair, but I think doing good to people's rather a risky thing. You can lay up a lot of trouble, for yourself as well as the people who're being done good to. And it's so hard to be sure that the good you're trying to do really is good, the best thing for that person, and the justification of the whole business is a bit——"

"I'm in favour of taking risks. There's far too much playing safe these days, it's ruining the country, all this stick-in-the-mud attitude. I believe in taking off my coat and getting on with the job."

"But, Mair, these are risks that involve other people. You're deciding what's best for them and then doing it, just like that. You don't give them a chance to——"

"If you'd done as much social work as I have, John, perhaps you'd have some idea of how many people there are in this world who are constitutionally incapable of knowing what's best for them. They're like children. You wouldn't let Eira be the judge of what was best for her, would you? You wouldn't let her put her hand in the fire to see if it was hot, would you?"

"No, of course not, but children aren't——"

"I know you think social work's something terribly complicated and difficult. Well, believe me, ninety or ninety-five per cent of the time it couldn't be simpler, at least making the right decision couldn't : getting it carried out is something else again, of course, but the actual decision's a piece of cake, because you're dealing with complete fools or complete swine or both. You'd think the same after a month in my job, I know you would."

"I hope not."

"Honestly, John, if people in general thought like you there wouldn't be any progress at all."

"No, there wouldn't, would there?"

At this fundamental point Mair steered the car to the kerb and stopped it, not, it transpired, in order to fight me but because we'd arrived. Facing us when we got out was a meagre row of shops: a newsagent's with a lot of advertisements written on postcards, a barber-cum-tobacconist, an outfitter's whose window stock alone would have outfitted a hundred middle-aged ladies in wool from head to foot, and a place that had no doubt once been a shop in the full sense but was now whitewashed to above eye level. This last establishment had to one side of it a door, recently painted a British Railways brown, and a bell which Mair rang. Then she took me by the arm and drew me a yard or two along the pavement.

I said: "What's this in aid of, then?" in what was supposed to be a bantering tone. Actually I was only half noticing; my mind was busy trying to decide what Mair's "you'd think the same after a month in the job" thing had reminded me of.

"You don't want to be in front of the front door of a house like this when they open it."

"Oh?" That was it: the veteran colonial administrator to the just-out-from-England colonial administrator. *We're all a bit pro-wog when we first get out here, my boy; it's only natural. Soon wears off, though, you'll find.* "Why not?"

"Well, the door opening makes the draught rush through the house, and the draught carries the bugs with it. You don't want them to land on you."

"You mean really bugs?" She had my full attention now.

"You don't want them to land on you."

"Hallo, Mrs. Webster, don't often see you up this way."

"Oh, good afternoon, Emrys, how are you?" Mair turned

animatedly towards the new arrival, a young police constable with a long, pale nose. "Wife all right?"

"Well, no, she hasn't been too grand, actually. They had her back in for three days' observation the week before last, and the doctor said——" His voice became indistinguishable, chiefly because he was lowering its pitch, but also because he was removing its source in the direction of the shop that had committed itself so wholeheartedly to the woollen garment. Mair retreated with him, nodding a fair amount. I was still feeling impressed by her bit of know-how about the bugs. Real front-line stuff, that.

"Yes, who's here, please?" This came from the now open front door, at which a small red-haired, red-faced man was standing.

"My name's Lewis."

"I don't know you. What you want here?"

I looked along the pavement to where Mair, nodding faster, was standing with her back to me. It must have had all the appearance of a furtive, sidelong, up-to-no-good look. Like a fool, I said: "I'm a friend of your wife's." As I said this, I smiled.

"Get out of here," the red-haired man bawled. He wore a red shirt. "Get out, you bastard."

"Look, it's all right, there's no need to——"

"Get out quick, you bastard." For the first time he saw Mair and the policeman, who were now approaching. "Mrs. Webster, hallo. And you, officer. Take away this bastard."

"Now calm down, Bent, nothing to get excited about. Mr. Lewis is with me. He and his wife have been very kind to Betty. He's come along with me to see how you all are. He's a friend of mine."

"Sorry, Mrs. Webster. Sorry, sir, very sorry."

"That's all right, Bent, Mr. Lewis doesn't mind. He knows you didn't mean anything. You just forget it. Now, can we come in?"

"Please, yes, come in."

"Bye-bye, Emrys, give Maureen my love. Tell her I'll pop in to see her in a day or two. And don't you worry. She's a good strong girl and with the better weather coming she'll soon pull round, I guarantee."

"Thank you very much, Mrs. Webster. Goodbye now."

Before he turned away I caught a glimpse of Emrys's face and was startled to see on it an expression of relief and gratitude, quite as if he'd just received an important reassurance of some kind. I followed Mair across the threshold, frowning and shaking my head at life's endless enigma.

Bugs or no bugs, the house revealed itself to me as not too bad. There were loose and cracked floorboards, but none missing, and no damp; the kitchen we penetrated to was dark all right, but it smelt no worse than stale; through its open door I could see a scullery with a row of clean cups hanging above the sink and a dishcloth spread over the taps to dry. One of the twins came into view in that quarter, took in the sight of visitors and doubled away again.

"Good afternoon, Betty," Mair was saying in her hospital-rounds manner. "My goodness, you have done well, haven't you? You really ought to be congratulated. You have made the place look nice."

She went on like that while I glanced round the place. It did look nice enough as far as it went, but that wasn't at all far. Most noticeably, there was an absence of the unnecessary things, the ornaments, the photographs and pictures, the postcards on the mantelpiece that every home accumulates. It was as if the moving men had just dumped the furniture down, leaving the small stuff to be unpacked later, only in this case there was nothing to unpack. Curtains perhaps fell into the category of the unnecessary, even, with a small single window like this one, of the excessive. They were of Betty's favourite lilac shade, and ranks of mauve personages, with sword and fan, periwig and towering hair-do, were doing a minuet on them. At this sight I felt pity stirring. Get back, you brute, I said internally, giving it a mental kick on the snout. Then I felt angry with a whole lot of people, but without much prospect of working out just who.

Mair was nearing her peroration. I looked covertly at Betty. Although no longer tarted up, she hadn't recovered the quiet, youthful air she'd had when I first saw her. She wore a grey cardigan which seemed designed to accentuate the roundness of her shoulders. The circles under her eyes weren't the temporary kind. She was staring up at Mair with the sarcastic patience of someone listening to a shaky alibi. Bent Arnulfsen, after standing about uneasily for a time, went out into the scullery and I heard water plunging into a kettle. Still talking, the old moral commando moved to follow him. "I just want to have a word with Bent a minute," she said, and shut the door behind her.

"Well, how are things?" I asked.

Betty glanced at me without friendliness, then away. "Okay," she muttered, picking at a hole in the cover of her chair.

"Your husband seems a nice chap."

"What you know about it, eh?"

"I'm only going on how he struck me."

"Aw, he's okay, I suppose. He's a good boy."

"There's a lot to be said for good boys."

"Suppose so."

"You seem to have settled down here nicely."

"Yeah."

"Jean and the children asked to be remembered to you, by the way."

To shrug both her shoulders would have meant heaving herself up from the chair back, so she made do with just shrugging the uppermost one. It was clear to me that there was nothing left of the cordiality of our last meeting, and no wonder. A man who had seen her when she was free was the last kind of person on earth who should have been allowed to see her now she was tamed. And in any contact not made on terms of equality the speech of one party or the other will fall almost inevitably into the accents and idioms of patronage, as I'd just heard my own speech doing. Severity is actually more respectful. But that wouldn't do here. Would anything? I said: "Do you ever miss the old life?"

"What you want to know for? What's it got to do with you?"

"Nothing. I was only asking."

"Well, don't ask, see? Mind your own bloody business, see? What you want to come here for anyway?"

"I'm sorry, Betty. I just came to see how you were getting on."

"Like old Webster, eh? Well I don't like people coming along to see how I'm getting on, see? I gets brassed off with it, see?"

As she got up from her chair to make her point more forcibly, the scullery door opened and Mair came back into the room. My sense of relief filled me with shame. Triumph swept over Betty's face at being about to do what she must have wanted to do for quite a time.

"Your husband certainly thinks the world of you, Betty," Mair led off. "He's been telling me——"

"Get out, you old cow," Betty shouted, blinking fast. "I doesn't want you here, see? I got enough to put up with with the bloody neighbours hanging over the fence and staring in the bloody windows and them buggers upstairs complaining. I got enough without you poking your bloody nose in, see? Just you piss off quick and leave me alone."

"Please, my dear, be quiet." Bent Arnulfsen had re-appeared in the scullery doorway. In one hand he held a brown enamel teapot, in the other the hand of one of the twins. "Mrs. Webster is kind. And this gentleman."

"You keep out of this, man. Go on, Webster, what you waiting for? I said get out, didn't I? Who do you think you are, that's what I'd like to know—poking your bloody nose in everywhere and telling every bugger what to do. You're beyond, you are, Webster. Bloody beyond. And as for you——" At the moment when Betty, who was now crying, turned to me, Mair looked at her wristwatch with a quick movement. "Who asked you to come snooping in, that's what I'd like to know," Betty started to say to me, but Mair cut in.

"I'm afraid we shan't be able to manage that cup of tea, Bent," she said interestedly; "I'd no idea the time was getting along like this. I must take Mr. Lewis off to his place of work or I shall get into trouble. I'll be in next week as usual and I'm sure things will have settled down by then. Goodbye, Betty; don't upset yourself, there's a good girl. Goodbye, Bent."

With another look at me, full of accusation, Betty blun-

dered out into the scullery and banged the door. Later I
thought how cruel it was that she'd been met by bland pre-
occupation instead of the distress or anger she'd longed to
provoke, that her brave show of defiance must have seemed
to her to have misfired. But at the time I only wanted to get
out before she came back.

Brushing aside Bent Arnulfsen's halting apologies, Mair
led me away. "Astonishing how predictable these girls are,"
she said as we drove off. "I'd seen that little lot coming for
some time. You usually get it sooner or later and afterwards
you often find you get on better than you did before. Sort
of clears the air in a way. Next week she'll be falling over
herself and holding on to my hand and going on about
'Oh, Mrs. Webster, how could I have said what I did, what
a pig I was to you, Mrs. Webster, and you so kind,' and not
being able to do enough for me. Not that that phase lasts
very long, either. No, there's no doubt about it, if you look
for thanks in this job you're wasting your time and letting
yourself in for a big disappointment. The approval of your
conscience is all the reward you ever get."

"Seen this?" my wife asked me later in the same year.

I took the local paper from her and read that Elizabeth
Grace Arnulfsen (19) had been sentenced to two months'
imprisonment for helping to burgle a café in Harrieston.
(The two men who'd been with her got longer sentences.)
Mrs. Mair Webster, it was further reported, had spoken
of her belief that Elizabeth Arnulfsen was weak-willed
rather than vicious and had been led astray by un-
desirable companions. She said this out of her thorough
knowledge of the girl's character, and had been thanked for
saying it.

"Well, I hope Mair's satisfied," I said, throwing the paper down.

"Don't be silly, you know she'll be very cut up. She's always done her best for Betty."

"Her worst, you mean."

"Don't talk so soft."

"Betty only burgled that place to get her own back."

"What, on Mair?"

"Yes, I should say it was chiefly on Mair. Not on society or any of that crap. As a method of not being the kind of person Mair wanted her to be."

"Mm. Sounds more like just high spirits to me. And according to what you told me Betty'd been breaking into places quite a time back."

"Not until Mair'd started licking her into shape."

"You're exaggerating the whole thing, John. What should have happened according to you, anyway? Betty going on being a tart?"

"Why not?"

"What about the twins and this Bent bloke?"

"Yes. No, she shouldn't have gone on being a tart, or couldn't or something. Pity in a way, though. She was enjoying herself."

"You don't know anything about it. I'm going to make supper."

"I know how not to deal with people like Betty. Shall I give you a hand?"

"No, you make the cocoa after. How do you stop people being tarts? How would you do it if it was you?"

"Always assuming I thought I ought to try. It's all a mess. It all needs going into."

"Who's going to go into it? You and Mair?"

"No, just me. What about that supper?"

I could picture Mair doing what she'd have called help-ing Betty through the ordeal, going to see her in prison, meeting her when she got out and at once settling down again to the by now surely hopeless task of inducing her to lead a normal life with her husband and children. And what would friend Lewis be up to while all this was going on? Getting boozed with his mates, having fantasies about some new beautiful borrower, binding about his extra even-ing duties in the summer and explaining to his wife that you couldn't have good social workers, because the only kind of chap who'd make a good one was also the kind of chap who'd refuse to be one. Of the two of us, it had to be admitted that on the face of it Mair had a claim to be con-sidered the less disreputable character, up there in the firing line while cowards flinched and traitors sneered.

Once you got off the face of it, though, and got on to what Mair was actually doing up there in the firing line, the picture changed a bit, just as things like the Labour Party looked better from some way away than close to. This was a timely reflection, because I'd been almost starting to admire Mair rather, and admiring someone you think is horrible is horrible. It was true enough that you had to have social workers, in the same way that you had to have prison warders, local government officials, policemen, military policemen, nurses, parsons, scientists, mental-hospital atten-dants, politicians and—for the time being anyway, God for-give us all—hangmen. That didn't mean that you had to feel friendly disposed towards any such person, bar the odd nurse perhaps, and then only on what you might call extrinsic grounds.

Actually, of course, it wasn't Mair I ought to have been

cogitating about. Mair, with her creed of take-off-your-coat-and-get-on-with-it (and never mind what "it" is), could be run out of town at any stage, if possible after being bound and gagged and forced to listen to a no-holds-barred denunciation of her by Betty. What if anything should or could be done about Betty, and who if anyone should or could do it and how—that was the real stuff. I was sorry to think how impossible it was for me to turn up at the gaol on the big day, holding a bunch of flowers and a new plastic umbrella.

INTERESTING THINGS

INTERESTING THINGS

Gloria Davies crossed the road towards the Odeon on legs that weaved a little, as if she was tipsy or rickety. She wasn't either really; it was just the high-heeled shoes, worn for the first time specially for today. The new hoop earrings swayed from her lobes, hitting her rhythmically on the jaws as she walked. No. They were wrong. They had looked fine in her bedroom mirror, but they were wrong, somehow. She whipped them off and stuffed them into her handbag. Perhaps there'd be a chance to try them again later, when it was the evening. They might easily make all the difference then.

She stopped thinking about the earrings when she found she couldn't see Mr. Huws-Evans anywhere in the crowd of people waiting for their friends on the steps of the Odeon. She knew at once then that he hadn't really meant it. After all, what could an Inspector of Taxes (Assessment Section) see in an eighteen-year-old comptometer operator? How stuck-up she'd been, congratulating herself on being the first girl in the office Mr. Huws-Evans had ever asked out. Just then a tall man who'd been standing close by took off his beige mackintosh hat with a drill-like movement, keeping his elbow close to his chest. It was Mr. Huws-Evans.

"Hallo, Gloria," he said. He watched her for a bit, a smile showing round the curly stem of the pipe he was biting. Then he added : "Didn't you recognise me, Gloria?"

"Sorry, Mr. Huws-Evans, I sort of just didn't see you." The hat and the pipe had put her off completely, and she was further confused by being called Gloria twice already.

He nodded, accepting her apology and explanation. He put his hat on again with a ducking gesture, then removed his pipe. "Shall we go in? Don't want to miss the News."

While Mr. Huws-Evans bought two two-and-fourpennies Gloria noticed he was carrying a string bag full of packets of potato crisps. She wondered why he was doing that.

It was very dark inside the cinema itself, and Mr. Huws-Evans had to click his fingers for a long time, and tremendously loudly, before an usherette came. The Odeon was often full on a Saturday when the football team was playing away, and Gloria and Mr. Huws-Evans couldn't help pushing past a lot of people to get to their seats. A good deal of loud sighing, crackling of sweet-packets and uncoiling of embraces marked their progress. At last they were settled in full view of the screen, on which the Duke of Edinburgh was playing polo. Mr. Huws-Evans asked Gloria loudly whether she could see all right, and when she whispered that she could he offered her a chocolate. "They're rather good," he said.

Almost nothing happened while the films were shown. The main feature was on first. As soon as Gloria could tell that it was old-fashioned she was afraid she wouldn't enjoy it. Nobody did anything in it, they just talked. Some of the talking made Mr. Huws-Evans laugh for a long time at a time, and once or twice he nudged Gloria. When he did this she laughed too, because it was up to her to be polite and

not spoil his pleasure. The film ended with a lot of fuss
about a Gladstone bag and people falling into each other's
arms in a daft, put-on way.

Gloria kept wondering if Mr. Huws-Evans was going to
put his arm round her. She'd never yet gone to the pictures
in male company without at least this happening, and
usually quite a lot more being tried on, but somehow Mr.
Huws-Evans didn't seem the man for any of that. He was
older than her usual escorts, to start with, and to go on with
there was something about that mackintosh hat and that
string bag which made it hard to think of him putting his
arm round anyone, except perhaps his mother. Once she
caught sight of his hand dangling over the arm of the seat
towards her, and she moved her own hand carefully so that
he could take hold of it easily if he wanted to, but he didn't.
He leaned rather closer to her to light her cigarettes than
he strictly needed to, and that was all.

After a pair of tin gates had been shown opening in a
slow and dignified way, there was about half an hour of
advertisements while everybody whistled the tunes that were
playing. The cereals and the detergents came up, then a
fairly long and thorough episode about razor-blades. During it Mr. Huws-Evans suddenly said: "It's a damned
scandal, that business."

"What's that, then?"

"Well, all this business about the modern shave. All these
damned gadgets and things. It's just a way of trying to get
you to use a new blade every day, that's all."

"Oh, I get you. You mean because the——"

"Mind you, with the kind of blade some of these firms
turn out you've got to use a new blade. I grant them that."
He laughed briefly. "If you don't want to skin yourself

getting the beard off, that is. And of course they don't give a damn how much they spend on publicity. It's all off tax. Doesn't really cost them a bean."

Gloria was going to say "How's that, then?" but Mr. Huws-Evans's manner, that of one with a comprehensive explanation on instant call, warned her not to. She said instead: "No, of course it doesn't."

He looked at her with mingled scepticism and wistfulness, and ended the conversation by saying violently: "Some of these firms."

While the lights went down again, Gloria thought about this brief exchange. It was just the kind of talk older men went in for, the sort of thing her father discussed with his butties when they called to take him down to the pub, things to do with the Government and pensions and jobs and the Russians, things that fellows who went dancing never mentioned. She saw, on the other hand, that that kind of talk wasn't only tied up in some way with getting old, it also had to do with having money and a car, with speaking properly and with being important. So a girl would show herself up for a lump with no conversation and bad manners if she gave away to an older man the fact that uninteresting things didn't interest her. Next time Mr. Huws-Evans got on to them she must do better.

The second film promised to be full of interesting things. There were some lovely dresses, the star looked just like another star Gloria had often wished she looked like, and there was a scene in a kind of flash night-club with dim lights, men in tail coats and a modern band. The star was wearing a terrific evening dress with sequins and had a white fur round her shoulders. A man with a smashing profile sitting at the bar turned and saw her. Her eyes met his for a long moment. Gloria swallowed and leant forward in her seat.

Mr. Huws-Evans nudged Gloria and said: "Don't think much of this, do you? What about some tea?"

"Oh, we haven't got to go yet, have we?"

"Well, we don't want to sit all through this, do we?"

Gloria recollected herself. "No, right you are, then."

They moved effortfully back along the row, taking longer this time because some of the embraces were slower in un-coiling. In the foyer, Gloria said: "Well, thank you very much, Mr. Huws-Evans, I enjoyed the film ever so much," but he wasn't listening; he was looking wildly about as if he'd just found himself in a ladies' cloakroom, and begin-ning to say: "The crisps. I've left them inside."

"Never mind, don't you worry, it won't take a minute fetching them. I don't mind waiting at all."

He stared out at her from under the mackintosh hat, which he'd pulled down for some reason so that it hid his eyebrows. "I shan't be able to remember the seat. You come too, Gloria. Please."

After a lot more finger-clicking inside they found the row. In the beam of the usherette's torch Gloria saw that their seats were already occupied. Even more slowly than before, Mr. Huws-Evans began shuffling sidelong away from her; there was some disturbance. Gloria, waiting in the aisle, turned and looked at the screen. The man with the profile was dancing with the star now and all the other people had gone back to their tables and were watching them. Gloria watched them too, and had forgotten where she was when a moderate uproar slowly broke out and slowly moved to-wards her. It was Mr. Huws-Evans with the crisps, which were rustling and crunching like mad. Men's voices were denouncing him, some of them loudly and one of the loud ones using words Gloria didn't like, in fact one word was the word she called "that word." Her cheeks went hot. Mr. Huws-Evans was saying things like "Very sorry, old boy" and "Hurts me as much as it hurts you," and every so often he laughed cheerily. Everywhere people were calling "Ssshh." Gloria couldn't think of anything to do to help.

A long time later they were outside again. It was clear at once that the rain had stopped holding off hours ago. Mr. Huws-Evans took her arm and said they'd better run for it, and that was what they did. They ran a long way for it, and fast too, so that the high heels were doing some terrible slipping and skidding. Opposite Woolworth's Gloria nearly did the splits, but Mr. Huws-Evans prevented that, and was just as effective when she started a kind of sliding football tackle towards a lady in bifocal glasses carrying a little boy. That was just outside Bevan & Bevan's, and Gloria didn't mind it much because she'd guessed by now that they were going to Dalessio's, a fairly flash Italian restaurant frequented by the car-owning classes—unless, of course, they were making for Cwmbwrla or Portardulais on foot.

There was a queue in Dalessio's and Gloria panted out the news that she was going to the cloakroom, where there was another, but shorter, queue. While she waited her turn she felt her hair, which must have been looking dreadful, and wondered about her face, to which she'd applied some of the new liquid make-up everyone was talking about. She was glad to find, in due time, that she hadn't been looking too bad. Touching up with the liquid stuff didn't quite provide the amazing matt finish the advertisements described, in fact she wondered if she didn't look a bit like one of the waxworks she'd seen that time in Cardiff, but there was no time to re-do it and it must surely wear off a little after a bit. She gazed longingly at the earrings in her bag, and at the new mascara kit, but these must certainly wait. Taking a last peep at herself, she reflected gratefully, as her father had often exhorted her to do, that she was very lucky to be quite pretty and have all that naturally curly naturally blonde hair.

Mr. Huws-Evans had a table for two when she joined him. He took the bag of crisps off her chair and laid them reverently at his side. Gloria thought he seemed very attached to them. What did he want them for, and so many of them too? It was a puzzle. Perhaps he guessed her curiosity, because he said: "They're for the party. They said I was to get them."

"Oh, I see. Who'll be there? At the party? You did tell me when you asked me, but I'm afraid I've forgotten."

"Not many people you'll know, I'm afraid. There'll be Mr. Pugh, of course, from Allowances, and his wife, and Miss Harry from Repayments, and my brother—you've met him, haven't you?—and my dentist and his, er, and his friend, and two or three of my brother's friends. About a dozen altogether."

"It sounds lovely," Gloria said. A little tremor of excitement ran through her; then she remembered about poise. She arranged herself at the table like one of the models who showed off jewellery on TV, and purposely took a long while deciding what to have when the waitress came, though she'd known ever since passing Bevan & Bevan's that she was going to have mixed grill, with French fried potatoes. She was soon so lost in thoughts of the party and in enjoying eating that it was like a voice in a dream when Mr. Huws-Evans said:

"Of course, the real difficulties come when we have to decide whether something's income or capital."

Gloria looked up, trying not to seem startled. "Oh yes."

"For instance," Mr. Huws-Evans went on, drawing a long fishbone from his mouth, "take the case of a man who buys a house, lives in it for a bit and then sells it. Any profit he might make wouldn't be assessable. It's capital, not income."

"So he wouldn't have to pay tax on it, is that right?"

"Now for goodness' sake don't go and get that mixed up with the tax on the property itself, the Schedule A tax."

"Oh yes, I've heard of that. There were some figures I——"

"That still has to be paid." He leaned forward in an emphatic way. "Unless the man is exempt, of course."

"Oh yes."

"Now it'd be much easier, as you can imagine, to catch him on the sale of several houses. But even then we'd need to show that there was a trade. If the chap simply buys them as investments, just to get the rents, well then you couldn't catch him if he sold out later at a profit. There'd be no trade, you see."

"No." Gloria swallowed a mushroom-stalk whole. "No trade."

"That's right." He nodded and seemed pleased, then changed his tone to nonchalant indulgence. "Mind you, even the profit on an isolated transaction could be an income profit. There was the case of three chaps who bought some South African brandy, had it shipped over here and blended with French brandy, and sold it at a profit. But the Court still said there was a trade. They'd set up a selling organisation."

"Ah, I get it."

"You'll be perfectly all right just so long as you remember that income tax is a tax on income."

Gloria felt a little dashed when Mr. Huws-Evans found nothing to add to his last maxim. She hadn't spoken up enough and shown she was taking an interest. He couldn't just go on talking, with nobody helping to make it a proper conversation. And yet—what could she have said? It was so hard to think of things.

Mr. Huws-Evans launched off again soon and she cheered up. He questioned her about herself and her parents and friends and what she did in the evenings. He watched her with his big brown eyes and tended to raise his eyebrows slowly when she got near the end of each bit she said. Then, before asking his next question, he'd let his eyes go vacant, and drop his jaw without opening his mouth at all, and nod slightly, as if each reply of hers was tying up, rather disturbingly, with some fantastic theory about her he'd originally made up for fun : that she was a Communist spy, say, or a goblin in human form. During all this he dismantled, cleaned, reassembled, filled and lit his pipe, finally tamping down the tobacco with his thumb and burning himself slightly.

At last it was time to go. In the street Gloria said : "Well, thank you very much, Mr. Huws-Evans, I enjoyed the food ever so much," but he wasn't listening; he was rubbing his chin hard with some of his fingers, and beginning to say : "Shave. Got to have a shave before the party. That blade this morning."

They boarded a bus and went a long way on it. Mr. Huws-Evans explained, quoting figures, that a taxi wasn't worth while and that he personally was damned if he was

going to lay out all that cash on a car simply to make a
splash and impress a few snobs. He paid the conductor with
coins from a leather purse that did up with two poppers.
This purse, Gloria thought, was somehow rather like the
mackintosh hat and the string bag with the crisps. After
doing up the purse and putting it safely away Mr. Huws-
Evans said that his digs, where the shave was going to happen, were quite near Mr. Pugh's house, which was where the
party was going to happen. He added that this would give
them just nice time.

They got off the bus and walked for a few minutes. The
rain had stopped and the sun was out. Gloria cheered up
again, and didn't notice at first when Mr. Huws-Evans suddenly stopped in the middle of the pavement. He was looking about in rather the same way as he'd done in the foyer
of the Odeon. He said: "Funny. I could have sworn."

"What's the matter, then?"

"Can't seem to remember the right house. Ridiculous of
me, isn't it? Just can't seem to remember at all."

"Not your digs it isn't, where you can't remember, is it?"

"Well yes, my digs. This is it. No, there's no TV aerial."

"Never mind, what's the number?"

"That's the silly part. I don't know the number."

"Oh, but you must. How ever do you manage with letters
and things? Come on, you must know. Try and think,
now."

"No good. I've never known it."

"What?"

"Well, you see, the landlady's got one of those stamp
things to stamp the address at the top of the notepaper and
I always use that. And then when I get a letter I just see it's
for me and that's all I bother about, see?" He said most of

this over his shoulder in the intervals of trying to see through some lace curtains. Then he shook his head and walked on, only to bend forward slightly with hands on knees, like a swimmer waiting for the starting-pistol, and stare at a photograph of a terrier which someone had arranged, thoughtfully turned outward, on a windowsill. "The number's got a three in it, I do know that," he said then. "At least I think so."

"How do you manage as a rule?"

"I know the house, you see."

Mr. Huws-Evans now entered a front garden and put his eye to a gap in the curtains. Quite soon a man in shirtsleeves holding a newspaper twitched the curtain aside and stood looking at him. He was a big man with hair growing up round the base of his neck, and you could guess that he worked at some job where strength was important. Mr. Huws-Evans came out of the garden, latching its gate behind him. "I don't think that's the one," he said.

"Come on, why not just knock somewhere and ask?"

"Can't do that. They'd think I was barmy."

Eventually Mr. Huws-Evans recognised his house by its bright red door. "Eighty-seven," he murmured, studying the number as he went in. "I must remember that."

Gloria sat in the sitting-room, which had more books in it than she'd ever seen in a private house before, and looked at the book Mr. Huws-Evans had dropped into her lap before going up to have his shave. It was called *Income Taxes in the Commonwealth*, and he'd said it would probably interest her.

She found it didn't do that and had gone to see if there were any interesting books in the bookcase when the door opened and an old lady looked in. She and Gloria stared at each other for about half a minute, and Gloria's cheeks felt hot again. The old lady's top lip had vertical furrows and there was something distrustful about her. She gave a few grunts with a puff of breath at the beginning of each one, and went out. Gloria didn't like to touch the bookcase now and told herself that the party would make everything worth while.

When Mr. Huws-Evans came back he had a big red patch on his neck. "These razor-blade firms," he said bitterly, but made no objection when Gloria asked if she could go and wash her hands. He even came to the foot of the stairs to show her the right door.

The liquid make-up looked fine, the mascara went on like distemper on a wall and the earrings were just right now. She only hoped her white blouse and rust cocktail-length skirt, the only clothes she had that were at all evening, were evening enough. When she came out the old lady was there, about thirty inches away. This time she gave more puffing grunts than before and started giving them sooner. She was still giving them when Gloria went downstairs. But then Mr. Huws-Evans, as soon as he saw her, jumped up and said: "You look absolutely stunning, Gloria," so that part was worth while.

After they'd left, what Gloria had been half-expecting all along happened, though not in the way she'd half-expected. It now appeared that they were much too early, and Mr. Huws-Evans took her into a park for a sit-down. Before long he said: "You know, Gloria, it means a lot to me, you coming out with me today."

This was hard to answer, so she just nodded.

"I think you're the prettiest girl I've ever been out with."

"Well, thank you very much, Mr. Huws-Evans."

"Won't you call me Waldo? I wish you would."

"Oh no, I don't think I could, really."

"Why not?"

"I . . . I don't think I know you well enough."

He stared at her with the large brown eyes she'd often admired in the office, but which she now thought looked soft. Sadly, he said : "If only you knew what I feel about you, Gloria, and how much you mean to me. Funny, isn't it? I couldn't have guessed what you were going to do to me, make me feel, I mean, when I first saw you." He lurched suddenly towards her, but drew back at the last minute. "If only you could feel for me just a tiny bit of what I feel for you, you've no idea what it would mean to me."

An approach of this kind was new to Gloria and it flustered her. If, instead of all this daft talk, Mr. Huws-Evans had tried to kiss her, she'd probably have let him, even in this park place; she could have handled that. But all he'd done was make her feel foolish and awkward. Abruptly, she stood up. "I think we ought to be going."

"Oh, not yet. Please. Please don't be offended."

"I'm not offended, honest."

He got up too and stood in front of her. "I'd give anything in the world to think that you didn't think too hardly of me. I feel such a worm."

"Now you're not to talk so silly."

When it was much too late, Mr. Huws-Evans did try to kiss her, saying as he did so : "Oh, my darling."

Gloria side-stepped him. "I'm not your darling," she said decisively.

After that neither spoke until they arrived at the house where the party was. Mr. Huws-Evans's daft talk, Gloria thought, was to be expected from the owner of that mackin-tosh hat—which he still wore.

When Mr. Huws-Evans's brother caught sight of her their eyes met for a long moment. It was because of him—she'd seen him once or twice when he called in at the office—that she'd accepted Mr. Huws-Evans's invitation. Originally she'd intended just to look at him across the room while she let Mr. Huws-Evans talk to her, but after what had happened she left Mr. Huws-Evans to unpack his crisps and put them in bowls while the brother (it was funny to think that he was Mr. Huws-Evans too, in a way) took her across the room, sat her on a sofa and started talking about interesting things.

ALL THE BLOOD WITHIN ME

ALL THE BLOOD WITHIN ME

THAT MORNING ALEC MACKENZIE had been unable
to eat even his usual small breakfast, so when, some minutes
out of Euston, coffee and light refreshments were announced, he went along to the dining-car. He felt that, in
view of what lay ahead, he should have something inside
him, however nasty it or the task of getting it down might
prove. It was good, too, to quit the company of those
sharing his compartment, a standard crew of secret agents
for the bus companies : two sailors and a portable radio, an
ever-toddling toddler, a man whose pipe whimpered and
grumbled, an old woman with a hat who moved her lips as
she read her library book and wet her fingers thoroughly
before turning each page.

The first person he saw on entering the dining-car was
Bob Anthony, wearing a suit that looked like woven vegetable soup and reading a newspaper with awful concentration. Alec found it hard not to dive back the way he had
come, let alone stand his ground, but he knew that the two
of them must have caught the train for the same reason and
would have to meet sooner or later. Hoping only that it
would be later, he did not resist when the steward put him
in a chair facing Bob's, but at the opposite end of the car.

For twenty-four hours now his brain had behaved as if some terminal had come loose, deactivating half of it and letting the rest work only at low efficiency. Perhaps this was what people meant when they talked about moving round in a trance. The half-rural landscape, wheeling past the window in average September sunshine, had a flat, pointless quality. Alec felt a slight amazement that things like keeping out of Bob's way for a few extra minutes should still matter to him, and again that he should find himself making his customary weak and futile appeal for a pot of tea instead of the donkey-coloured mixture now being served under the name of coffee. Habit persisted when other things broke down. He drank coffee and ate biscuits.

The one look he had had at Bob had been quite enough to assure him that Bob's recent outbreak of affluence showed no sign of abating. Alec was well enough resigned to his own failure—bowing uncomplainingly to the inevitable was part of his code—but he had no intention of ceasing to be indignant at Bob's luck. A long period of floundering round the legal profession had been halted by two deaths. The first of these, brought on by an alcoholic seizure occurring slightly ahead of expectation, had had the effect of hauling Bob up a notch or two; the second, in which drink had played a more devious role as the agent of a fall downstairs, had made him virtual head of the firm, Bob having helped fate along, so to speak, by becoming friendly with the faller's widow. The depth of this friendship remained obscure, but it was certain that the second dead man's half-share in the business had passed under Bob's control and stayed there.

An approaching disturbance—the sound of a hip striking the corner of a laden table, the clash of crockery on a tray abruptly snatched from collision—warned Alec that Bob was on his way to join him. He looked up and saw that, apart from some lateral distortion caused by the movement of the train, the old stooping gait was the same as ever, not in the least scholarly, the tread of someone closing in on bodily enjoyment or the means to buy some.

"Hallo, Mac," Bob said in his curt tone and fake-genteel accent, then at once set about making people move so that he could sit where he wanted, opposite Alec. When he had done this he swept the cloth with the edge of his newspaper and they looked at each other in a way they often did, Bob unconcernedly claiming superior sophistication, Alec on the defensive, ready, if challenged, to stress the importance of moral fibre. Then both turned blank and grim. Alec found nothing to say; his attention was like a weight too heavy to move from where it had landed, on Bob's suit. Why was he wearing it? He must have others. Where were they?

"Well, Mac, words aren't much use at a time like this, eh?"

"No. No, they're not."

Bob signalled emphatically for more coffee. "I'd have thought you'd have gone down there yesterday."

"I didn't like to intrude."

"Oh, but surely, I mean Jim would have been glad to have you there, old chap. After all, you're not exactly a stranger."

"I worked it out that he'd sooner have been on his own. I know I would if it had been me."

"That's where you go wrong, Mac, if I may say so. You're by way of being a reserved type, always have been. I'm not blaming you, heaven knows—you can't help the way you're made—but most people aren't like that, you see. They want their pals round them. I call that a normal human instinct. Tell me, are you still living at that place of yours in Ealing?"

"You asked me that the last time you saw me in the Lord Nelson. I haven't moved since then."

"It would drive me crackers, quite frankly, being on my own twelve hours of the day. What do you do when you feel like nipping out and having a few?"

"I haven't got much cash for nipping out and having a few, so the question doesn't arise very often."

"No, I see." Bob seemed not to have noticed the bitterness which Alec had been unable to keep out of his voice. Not noticing things like that was no doubt useful to one who led Bob's kind of life. After gazing with apparent incredulity at the coffee with which their cups were now being refilled, he went on : "What do you do of an evening, then? You can't just——"

"Oh, I get a bit of bridge now and again, and there are one or two people I drop in on. There's a colleague of mine in the export department living just ten minutes' walk away. I usually have some grub with him and his wife Sunday midday and occasionally in the week."

"Still go to your concerts?"

"Not so much now."

Bob shook his head and drew in his breath. "It wouldn't do for me, I must say."

"Well, we're not all built the same, are we?"

"No, I like being in company."

Alec knew how true this was. The advent of the partner's widow had done nothing to curb Bob's habit of suddenly appearing in the Lord Nelson, the pub near the Temple both men were apt to use at lunch-time, and plying some woman with large gin-and-frenches while Alec sat up at the bar with his light ale and veal-and-ham pie and salad. Every few minutes the other two would burst out laughing at some trivial phrase, or go off into face-to-face mumbling that sometimes led to more laughter, all eyes and teeth. He never knew how to behave during these interludes.

The train had stopped at a station. Bob glanced out of the window and dropped his voice slightly. "I suppose it was another stroke, was it? Jim wasn't very clear on the phone."

"Yes, it was a stroke all right. She died before they could get her to hospital."

"Good way to go, I suppose. Better than poor old Harry. He was under drugs for almost a year, you know. It makes you wonder what sort of exit you'll have when it comes to your turn. Selfish, of course, but natural. Do you ever think about that, Mac? How you'll go?"

"Yes."

"Still, there's no use getting morbid. Actually I should think of the two of us you'll last longest. You thin little wiry chaps take a devil of a lot of killing, in my experience. You're a bit younger than me anyway, aren't you?"

"I was sixty-four in June."

"Not six months in it. We don't live to much of an age in our family. Harry was the same age as me when he snuffed it, and then poor Dora was barely fifty, and now here's Betty only sixty-seven; well, I say 'only,' that's not really old as things go nowadays, is it? Still, look at it another way and it's a lot of years. You must have known her since, what, 'thirty-two or -three?"

"The ... I'm not sure of the date, but it was August Bank Holiday, 1929."

"Here, that's pretty good card-index work, Mac. Well I'm blowed. How on earth do you remember it so exactly?"

"It was the day of the mixed doubles tournament at that tennis club near Balham we all used to belong to." Alec began filling his pipe. "I got brought in to run the show at the last minute. Until the Friday I didn't see how there could be a show, and what with the teas to arrange and one thing and another it'll be a long time before I forget that day, believe me."

"Mm. It, er, turned out all right, did it?"

"Yes, Betty and Jim got into the semi-finals. Nobody knew if they were any good or not, with them just moving into the district. But then they took the first set 6-1, and everyone could see ... well, as soon as Betty had made her first couple of shots, really. Her backhand was very strong, unusual in a woman. I didn't get a chance against them myself, because ..."

As clearly as if he had just seen a photograph of it, Alec recalled one moment of that first day. Jim, his bald head gleaming in the sun, was standing up at the net; Betty had stepped forward from the baseline and, with as much control as power, was sending one of her backhand drives not more than an inch or two above the net and squarely between their two opponents, who formed the only blurred patches in the image. Although the farthest away, Betty's figure was well defined, the dark hair in a loose bob, the sturdy forearms and calves, the straight nose that gave her face such distinction, even the thinning of the lips in concentration and effort. Some details were wrong—Betty's pleated white skirt belonged not to that afternoon, Alec knew, but was part of a summer dress she had worn on a day trip to Brighton just before the war, and Jim had not been so bald so early. There was nothing to be done about it, though: while a part of his mind fumbled left-handedly

to correct it, the picture stayed as it was. Just as well, perhaps, that it had not been given to human beings to visualise things at will.

Long before Alec was finally silent, Bob was glancing
fitfully about, extending and shortening his body and neck
like someone trying to see over a barrier that constantly
varied in height. He was always having to have things:
another round of drinks, the right time, a taxi, the menu,
the bill, a word with old So-and-so before they settled down.
While he twitched a nose rich in broken capillaries, he said
inattentively: "Of course, you were pretty attached to her,
weren't you, Mac?"

"Yes, I was."

"And so was she to you, old thing." The distance between
Bob's waist and chin grew sharply, as if a taxi-driver or
possibly a racing tipster had flung himself down full length
behind Alec's seat. "She was always on about you, you
know. Talking about you."

"Really?"

"Oh yes. You had a lot of brains, according to her.
Looked up to you, so she said. I'd like a miniature of
brandy, please," he added over Alec's shoulder. "Wait a
minute. Better make it two."

Alec began wondering how to decline the offer of a
miniature of brandy. He need not have worried, because
when they came Bob put them both carefully away in the
pockets of the woven-soup suit. He then tried to pay for
Alec's coffee, but Alec prevented him.

"Ah, we're just coming in," Bob said: "there's that
pickle-factory place. Appalling stink when the wind's in the
right direction, makes you wonder what they put in the
blessed stuff. How are you feeling, old chap?"

"Me? I'm perfectly all right." The barrier in Alec's head had given no sign of breaking down in the last five minutes, which meant it might just possibly stay in position for the next three hours, or however long it was going to be before he could decently leave. If he could hold out until then, the truth about him and Betty would never be known to any outsider, especially Bob. The thought of their secret being turned over by that parvenu mind, frivolous, hard-headed and puritanical in turn, and never the right one at the right time, was unendurable.

Bob had got up and was looking at his watch. "Good for you, Mac. Mm, late as per usual. I think we'd better go straight to the church. It might be the best thing in some ways."

"Will you sit, please," the clergyman directed. He was a bulky man of about fifty-five with white hair carefully combed and set. He had a thick voice, as if his throat were swollen. It went down a tone or two each time he told the congregation to change its posture. His way of doing this even when it was clearly unnecessary, and of giving every such syllable its full value, made up a good substitute for quite a long sentence about the decline of church-going, the consequent uncertainty and uneasiness felt by many people on such occasions as did bring them into the house of God, his own determination that there should be no confusion in his church about what some might think were small points of procedure, and the decline of church-going. Now, after making absolutely certain that everyone had done his bidding, he pronounced the dead woman's name in the manner of an operator beginning to read back a telegram.

"Elizabeth ... Duerden," he said, "has brought us together here today by virtue of the fact that she has recently died. I need not tell you that the death of someone we love, or even the death of any human being, is the most serious and important event with which this life can confront us. I want for a short time, if I may, to look into this business of death, to suggest a little of what it is, and of what it is not. I believe that the loss which her ... family has suffered is not absolute, that that thing exists which we so frequently name and seek and offer, so rarely define and obtain and give, that there is consolation, if only we know where to look for it. Where, then, are we to look?"

By now the man sounded as if he had been going on for hours and had more hours ahead of him. Some of the thickness, however, had left his voice when he continued: "In another age than ours, we should find it natural to look in the first place to the thought that to be separated from the ones we love by the death of the body is not final. We should derive our consolation from knowing that no parting is for ever, that all losses will, in God's good time, be restored. But that would hardly do today, would it, thinking along those lines? It wouldn't do much for most of us today."

Something so close to vigour had entered the speaker's tone in the last couple of sentences that they were like an interruption, from which he himself took a moment to recover. Then he went on as thickly as ever: "But God's mercy has seen to it that we need not depend for our consolation upon any such belief. We find this out as soon as we can put aside something of our agony and shock and begin to ask ourselves what has happened. What has happened is manifestly that somebody has been taken from us and nothing will ever be the same again. But what has not happened? That person has not been eradicated from our

hearts and minds, that person's life has not been cancelled
out like a row of figures in a sum, that person's identity is
not lost, and can never be lost. . . . Elizabeth Duerden lives
in those who knew her and loved her. The fact that she
lived, and was Elizabeth Duerden and no one else, had a
profound effect upon a number of people, a considerable
effect upon many more people, a slight but never
imperceptible effect upon innumerable people. There is
nobody, there never has been anybody, of whom it can be
said that the world would have been the same if they had
never lived."

He can string words together, Alec thought. Or whoever
had written the stuff could. He looked round the church,
anxious to impress on his memory this part, at least, of today. But it was a modern building, thirty years old at the
most, with bright stained glass, a tiled floor, and woodwork
that reminded him of the dining-room suites he saw in
suburban shop windows: none of the air of antiquity that
had always appealed to Betty.

The Gioberti family occupied the pew in front. The farthest away from him was Annette Gioberti, who turned her
head now and gave him a faint smile. The bearer of this
exotic name looked like a soberly but becomingly dressed
English housewife in her middle thirties, which, as the
daughter of Jim and Betty, was much what might have
been expected of her. Jim had been against the marriage at
first, saying among other things that, while he had no objection to Italians or half-Italians as such, he did not fancy
having his grandchildren brought up as Roman Catholics.
But Betty had soon laughed him out of that by asking him
when he had last had anything to do with the Church of
England, and had added that Frank Gioberti was a decent,

hard-working lad who was obviously going to do everything in his power to make Annette happy—what more could they ask?

Alec had never known Betty to err in her judgments of people, and in this case she had turned out to be almost too literally accurate. From what she told Alec, whose direct contacts with the Giobertis were rare, there was plenty of money around in that household, and no shortage of affection, especially if you counted the more obvious kind of show of it—expensive presents on anniversaries as well as birthdays, and bunches of flowers being delivered unexpectedly. But as regards the finer things of life (Alec always wanted to smile at this favourite phrase of Betty's, so characteristic of her in its naïve sincerity) there was a complete gap: no books apart from trashy thrillers, no music except what the wireless and gramophone churned out, and no pictures at all; in fact Betty had given them a Medici print of a mediaeval *Virgin and Child* one Christmas, thinking it would appeal to Frank, and had come across it months later in a drawer in one of the children's bedrooms.

The part of Frank that could be seen above the back of the pew seemed to Alec to offer a good deal of information. The thick black hair was heavily greased; the neck bulged in a way that promised a roll of fat there in due course; the snowily white shirt-collar and the charcoal-grey suit material did somehow or other manage to suggest, not lack of taste exactly, but the attitude that money was more interesting. Still, one had to be tolerant. A man who owned however many laundries it was in the Deptford area could hardly be expected to have the time or the inclination to take up the French horn. It was only the children who might be the losers, especially since, in a materialistic age like the present one, the parent had a special responsibility for suggesting that there were some worthwhile things which nobody could be seen eating or drinking or smoking or wearing or driving or washing dishes in on TV commercials. And then people wondered why there was all this....

Alec pulled himself physically upright in his seat. It was almost frightening, the way the mind could so easily follow its well-worn tracks, even at times of unique stress. Habit again: nature's protection. He turned cold at the thought that today might pass him by altogether, that he might in some way miss experiencing it or beginning to understand it. The most abject and revealing loss of composure would be better than that. He started doing what he could never have predicted: trying to feel. "A human being," the clergyman was saying, "is the sum of many qualities, and it is from what we see of these that we form our ideas of what everything in life is, of what life itself is." No help there. Alec glanced over to the front pew across the aisle, where Jim and Bob sat together. With the Giobertis, this was all the family there was. Jim's brother, who had emigrated to Canada getting on for thirty years ago, had not received Jim's cable, or had not answered it, and it was now nearly twenty years—yes, twenty next April—since young Charlie, Annette's brother, had been killed in a motor-cycle accident in Alexandria, three weeks after getting his commission in the Royal Armoured Corps. Well, he had been spared all this.

Jim's face, half-turned towards the clergyman, looked quite relaxed, and he had seemed so in the brief moment at the church door when Alec had just had time to grasp his hand and murmur a few words, though his movements and reactions had been a little slower than usual. It had been the same, Alec remembered, the night the telegram about Charlie arrived. He had got there in the small hours —he had left his digs within a minute of getting Jim's phone call, but the train had been held up by an air alert —to find Betty in a state of collapse, naturally, and Jim simply being Jim, only more so: calm, solid, desperately hurt but not defeated, saying little as always, showing a degree of strength that even Alec, who admired him more than any other man he had ever met, had not expected. Thank God that Jim, at least, was still here. Now that he was alone, Jim might well consider throwing in his lot with him, sharing some sort of household, even perhaps (Alec put this part of his thought aside for future reference) coming into the small glass-merchandising firm of Keith Mackenzie and Company in which Alec, upon his retirement next year, was planning to join his brother Iain. If that appealed to Jim, it would be a kind of continuation of the Trio—the name Alec used in his own mind for the unit the Duerdens and he had comprised for over thirty years. And it would be a fine memorial to Betty.

"And so to have lived in vain," Alec heard the clergyman say, "is inconceivable." Even the thickest and most preternaturally apathetic voices have a directional component, and Alec became half-aware that this one was being beamed towards him. When a pause followed, he looked up and saw that the clergyman was indeed staring angrily into his face. After another second or two of ocular reprimand, the man spoke again. He was plainly drawing to a close, and now the hint of a new tone was heard, the detached disgust of a schoolmaster reading out to his class some shameful confidential document he has snatched from the hot hand of one of their number.

"Whence do we derive our ideas of what is most precious and admirable and lovable in human nature? Not from any inborn knowledge, but from what we see in those around us. To know somebody, and even more to know them with love, is constantly to be made aware of what human nature is and can be. To have known somebody with love is to be permanently illuminated with the human capacity for tenderness, for generosity, for gaiety, for disregard of self, for courage, for forgiveness, for intelligence, for compassion, for loyalty, for humility—and nobody has ever lived who has been unable to offer his fellow-creatures some one or other of these. And is this illumination an aspect of life, a side of life, a part of life? No, it is life itself, this learning what we are. And can death diminish that? No, death can do nothing with it, death even throws it into prominence, death is cheated. As death will always be cheated. Let us pray. Will you kneel, please."

Alec knelt and tried to pray, but could not decide what to pray to. The principle for good he sometimes thought of as existing above and beyond everything, and which he had expected (wrongly) to become more real to him as he grew older, seemed to involve a way of looking at things that included a belief in Betty's having a future, and he could not see how she could have any. So he made some wishes about the past instead, that Betty had had a happy life and had not suffered when she was dying. He felt his mind slowing down and becoming a blank, and would have begun to forget where he was if it had not been for the diminishing footfalls that told him he was about to be left alone. He got quickly to his feet and hurried outside.

Jim was shaking hands with the last group of local people

under the eye of the clergyman, whose manner now implied that he had been forced into his vestments as part of a practical joke and could see, for the moment, no dignified way of extricating himself. He looked bigger, too.

Alec felt impelled to speak to him: "Thank you for your address, Vicar, I thought it was most——"

"Rector," the other said, moving off.

"Right, let's get on, Mac," Jim said. "Who are you going up with?"

There were only two cars to be seen, one with Bob in it, the other full of Giobertis. "Oh, don't worry about me," Alec said rather wildly. "I can walk. How do I get to the——?"

"Nonsense, hop in with me and Bob."

"No, that's for the . . . I wouldn't want to——"

"Well then, go with Annette and Frank and the kids. These buses take five easily."

"In here, Uncle Mac," Annette called, and began making a place for him between herself and her husband. The two Gioberti girls occupied the folding seats: Sonia, a bespectacled blonde child of seven or eight with, so far as could be made out, a perfectly spherical head, and Elizabeth, a somewhat darker fourteen-year-old with a figure which, Alec supposed, many grown women would envy. As they moved off, she asked: "Where did you leave the car, Pop?"

Frank answered in his strong cockney accent: "Outside that hotel where we're going to have lunch, the King's Head or whatever it's called. Tumbledown-looking joint."

"Why couldn't we have gone up to the cemetery in our car?"

"Because we're going up in this one."

"Why? Ours is much more comfortable."

"I dare say it is, but we're going up in this one and that's an end of it, see?"

"What are we going up to the cemetery for?" Sonia asked.

"To see Gran being buried."

"It won't hurt her," Sonia stated.

"Of course it won't hurt her, she's dead."

"What are we going up to see her being buried for?"

"Because that's what we do."

"Sonia, take your shoes off there," Annette said.

"And shut up," Frank added.

"How's Christopher?" Alec asked. "Let's see, he must be nearly——"

"He was four in June."

"Really? It seems only the other——"

"Auntie Gina's looking after him today," Elizabeth said with a hint of triumph. "Over at Camberwell."

To forestall another invitation to silence from Frank, Alec looked out of the window. His eyes immediately fell on the little coffee shop with green check curtains where, whenever he came down for the weekend, he and Betty would spend an hour or so on the Saturday morning before strolling along to the King's Head to meet Jim after his morning of local activities—work for the Ratepayers' Association or the Golf Club committee—and relaxing over a couple of pink gins in the saloon bar, followed by lunch under the low beamed ceiling of the dining-room. It was at times like that that the Trio had really come into its own again, and for days and weeks afterwards there would be a lifting of the shadow that had fallen over Alec's life since

1945. With the war over, the Duerdens had decided to stay
on in this part of Buckinghamshire, where they had come
in 1941 as a temporary measure to avoid the bombing, and
not return after all to their house in Clapham. Since he
could not reciprocate their hospitality, Alec had had to
confine himself to staying with them only half a dozen times
a year at the outside, and had seen them hardly more often
for a meal or a theatre in London. He supposed he ought
to be thankful that the Trio had survived as well as it had,
that it had ever been able to recapture the spirit of its hey-
day, those twelve happiest years of his life between 1929
and 1941 when the Duerdens and he had occupied
houses facing the Common, not four hundred yards
apart.

Alec's face was still turned towards the window, but he
saw nothing of the neat residential area, its pavements
decorated with a staked lime sapling every fifty feet,
through which they were now passing. He was thinking of
the moment when he had first named the Trio to himself.
He and two or three other people (he forgot who) had
taken their music round to the Duerdens' one Sunday evening and, after the coffee and tomato sandwiches, Jim had
asked him to have a shot at the accompaniment of a duet
they had bought recently. He had sat down at the piano,
which had an excellent tone for an upright, and played the
thing for them at sight, something of a feat with such bold,
dramatic writing, full of shifting trills in both hands. It was
"Onaway, Awake, Beloved," a far more interesting setting
than that in Coleridge-Taylor's *Hiawatha*, which he had
always thought—secretly, for Betty delighted in it, and had
met the composer once at a wedding in Croydon—a bit of a
bore. Out of the corners of his eyes Alec had been able to

see both Betty and Jim as they sang, and when, with his
support, the two voices swept into

Does not all the blood within me
Leap to meet thee, leap to meet thee,
As the springs to meet the sunshine,
In the moon when nights are brightest?

he had felt his own blood leaping through him in a strange,
painful rhythm, as if he had stumbled on a mysterious
secret. And so he had; he had discovered that there could
be a relationship between three people for which none of
the ordinary words—friendship, love, understanding, intim-
acy—would quite do. When the song finished there had
been enthusiastic applause from the others, even from ten-
year-old Charlie, who was staying up late as a special treat,
and Alec's excitement had passed unnoticed.

The car stopped outside the cemetery. Although Alec had
walked along most of the roads in the area many times in
the last twenty years, the exterior of this place, and its whole
location, were totally unfamiliar to him.

"Here we are," Frank said. "Want any help, Uncle
Mac?"

"No thank you."

He got out and began walking towards the graveside,
remembering that, outside his family and their circle, Betty
was the only person who had ever called him "Alec," and
she only for a brief period, perhaps a year after their first
meeting. Then she had slipped into calling him "Mac" as
everyone else did, or rather as Jim in particular did. With
that fine tact of hers, the finer for being unselfconscious, she
had made it clear that there was not to be even the slightest
and most nominal acknowledgment of what she felt for

Alec, just as he had never by a single word acknowledged what he felt for her. The idea that two people could fall in love instantly and irrevocably and never mention it, let alone do anything about it, would have seemed incomprehensible or lunatic to anybody but themselves, or rather, again, to anybody but themselves and Jim. For Jim had somehow made it clear to Alec that he knew, but without hurt or resentment; he knew, but he understood and forgave, and so made it possible for Alec to go on seeing them without losing his self-respect. It was silently agreed between the three of them that while she loved Jim no less, she loved Alec too with a different—he recoiled from the mental impertinence of wondering if it were a deeper— kind of love. Few women would have been capable of that, but love had been Betty's gift.

Alec answered an imaginary question about what he had done with his life by saying to himself that he had loved a fine woman and known a true friend. The love came first, as love must. By repeating this slowly he succeeded for a time in shutting out the presence of those standing near him and all but the first phrase of the dreadful words the clergyman was saying. Then Alec started noticing the coffin lying in the grave. It had been lowered by means of green straps that recalled to him, in their colour and texture, the webbing belt Charlie Duerden had worn with his uniform when they lunched at Simpson's together during one of the boy's leaves. A handful of earth was thrown on to the coffin. Alec realised that he had been very afraid of the hollow noise this might make, but it was all right, the soil was dry and chalky, without noticeable clods, and when the spades got to work it could, from the sound, have been anything at all being buried. There were the beginnings of movement away

from the graveside; Alec sighed and raised his head, and
the whole scene shone brightly in his eyes : the people with
their varied complexions and hair, the grass, the privet
hedges, the vases of red and blue flowers on the graves, the
great pair of cypresses by the entrance, all slightly over-
coloured like a picture postcard. In the middle of it all Alec
saw the clergyman, looked squarely at him for the first time
since leaving the church, and saw that the clergyman, as
earlier, was looking at him.

The next moment after Alec felt he was going to cry he
started crying; he could no more have prevented it than he
could have prevented himself from gasping if a bucket of
icy water had been thrown over him. How did it help the
dead to have made the living aware of certain things? What
good to anyone were *ideas* about lovable qualities? What
use was it to *learn* about tenderness? What could you *do*
when you were illuminated about human possibilities, except
go round telling yourself how illuminated you were? What
was *knowing* in aid of? And what was it to *have loved*
someone?

"Here we go, old chap," Bob's voice said. "Just let's take
a little stroll together. That's right, steady as she goes. I was
wondering when you were going to crack. I was saying to
myself, I wonder when old Mac's going to crack. That's
your trouble, if I may say so, old stick : you keep things
bottled up too much. Far better let 'em come out, like this.
Well, you've picked the right time. Just a minute."

Alec became aware of the curious hooting noise he was
making, and pressed his hands over his mouth. "Nuisance,"
he said. "Sorry."

"Don't talk unmitigated piffle, old thing. Holler away for
a couple of hours if you feel like it. *Get rid of it.* Emotion

has got to come out. Sooner or later it's got to come out. That's human nature. Here. Go on, knock it back. Down in one. I'll join you if I may. I knew these little beggars would come in handy. Expensive way of buying booze, but still."

"Thirty years for nothing," Alec said, coughing. "Wasted my time."

"Oh no you haven't, Mac. People who've really done that don't mind. Here's the gate."

"No, pipe down, I'm doing this," Frank said loudly. "Mrs. Allen—another grapefruit juice? Sure you don't want anything stronger? Mrs. Holmes, what about you? Are you quite sure? Mrs. Higginbotham? Ah, that's more like it. Another for you, darling? Right. Now, Rector...large Scotch...Bob...large brandy and soda...Mr. Walton?"

Mr. Walton, the undertaker, said he would have a pint of black-and-tan with Guinness and best bitter. A tall, vigorous young man in his middle thirties, he had the look of a woodcutter or hedger momentarily in town to get his implements sharpened. Part of this look derived from his heavy tan, which had been acquired, so he explained earlier, during a recent five-week holiday on the Costa Brava. Alec found he could imagine Mr. Walton paying for an extra lavish sea-food dinner with one-sixth, say, of the profit on a moderately lavish funeral.

The party, some fifteen strong, was sitting or standing about in the lounge of the King's Head. Alec had been relieved at this choice of venue, thinking that the saloon bar at the side of the building would have been too full of associations, but a glance inside soon after arrival had shown him that, since his last visit here, the room had been so remodelled that he had been unable even to locate the nook by the vanished fireplace where he and Betty and Jim had drunk their pink gins not five Saturdays ago. All the horse-brasses and sporting prints, the uneven dark woodwork and frosted-glass panels that had given the bar its character had been swept away, and the new bright plastics made it bare and unwelcoming. Alec recognised this as part of a pattern of change. The things with which his life had been furnished—the tennis club, the Liberal Association and its strong social side, keeping up with the new plays, music in the sense he understood it, even such numerically unimportant occasions as George V's funeral and George VI's coronation—were no longer there.

The young waiter in the smart white jacket carried his tray over to where Alec was standing in silence with Jim. "I wanted to say how sorry I am, sir. We shall all miss Mrs. Duerden coming in here. We all liked her very much."

"Thank you, Fred, that's very nice of you. I think this is yours, Mac."

Alec took the whisky and soda. He had asked Frank for a small one, but its quantity, combined with the darkness of its colour, suggested that it was not very small. This would be his third double, not counting the brandy at the cemetery. Taking a hearty swallow, he tried for a moment to work out how much it was going to cost him to buy a round, then gave up. He could manage it, but it was a good job he had had the foresight to cash that three-quid cheque last night at his local. Much more important was the question of saying something meaningful to Jim, which he had not managed to do so far. He tried again: "I know this must seem like the end of everything, but it isn't really, you must believe that."

"Isn't it? Must I? I'm seventy years old, Mac. What am

I supposed to start doing at my age? It's just a matter of waiting now."

"Well, of course, that's how it seems, but——"

"No, that's how it is. Probably in a few months, I don't know, it'll look different again, but how, I just can't——"

"You'll find so many things you want to do."

"Look, you're not going to waffle about developing new interests, are you? Spare me that. Did I tell you that part-time job of mine with those varnish and stain people packs up at Christmas? What do I take up then? Chess?"

"There's bound to be something." Alec was disconcerted by the violence of Jim's tone and manner. He repressed an impulse to glance over his shoulder. Before he left he would mention to his friend the possibility of their joining forces in London, but now was clearly not the time.

"Oh yes, I'm sure," Jim said bitterly. "Wherever you look there's something. Oh, are you off, Rector? Haven't you got time for another one?"

"Unfortunately not." The clergyman spoke with feeling so intense as to be unidentifiable. "I have to be getting along."

"Well, you've been very kind and I'm most grateful." Jim turned aside to say goodbye to one of the local couples.

The clergyman looked at Alec. "Thank you for saying you liked my address," he said, blankly this time. "It's the one I . . . You're not family, are you?"

"No, just a friend."

"It's the one I use for those who have become members of my flock retroactively, so to speak—a proportion that increases every year."

"I see. It was you who——?"

The half-question hung in the air for a second or two

while what was arguably a smile modified parts of the clergyman's face. "Yes," he said, "alone and unaided I did it. But of course I was a much younger man then. Goodbye to you."

Soon afterwards they went in to lunch, just the family and Alec, five adults and two children. They sat at the round table in the window well away from the alcove favoured by the Trio: another relief. Further, Alec considered, it looked as if he were going to get away with not having to go up to the house at all. He wanted never to see it again, marked throughout as it was by Betty's personality— apart from such details as the oversized TV set Frank had had delivered on the Duerdens' fortieth wedding anniversary.

Their waiter offered his condolences, then the head waiter and the wine waiter; Frank caught the last-named by the sleeve before he could move away and ordered another round of drinks and two bottles of hock off him. The manager came over and chatted for a couple of minutes. He was a new man and had not known the Duerdens well, but, without pushing himself forward, he spoke the language of decent feeling. "I had hoped to get to the church this morning," he said, "but I just couldn't, with the Business Circle lunch and a christening party out of the blue. But I was thinking about you." Before departing he added: "Mrs. Duerden'll be missed all over the town. It won't be the same place without her."

This moved Alec in a gentle, unagonising way. Betty would never have wanted to be thought one of the important people in the district, but she had been a well-liked queen of her modest bits of castle. Such reflections occupied him for most of the meal, which soon began to acquire some sort of festive air. A couple of stories from Frank about the difficulties of bringing the laundry business up to date contributed little, Alec considered, apart from additional light on the fellow's character. When Bob got going, however, with what he called some unofficial law reports, it had to be admitted that he cheered everybody up. Even Jim had to laugh a few times, and the two Gioberti girls, each clutching a glass of pop, seemed spellbound.

While Alec ordered a round of liqueurs, Frank leaned back and lit a cigarette. "Fantastic really," he said. "Here we are, the lot of us, all having a good time, and two hours ago we were all, well, overwhelmed by grief. It just shows you, don't it? I mean it's natural, see? The church, the graveyard, the pub. Whoever it was thought up how to run funerals knew his job. I reckoned the service was real nice, didn't you, Ann?"

Annette kept her eyes on the table. "Very nice," she said.

"It was a bit, what shall I say? austere, that's the only criticism I got. Of course, you don't want to listen to us, we're Romans, we go for a bit of, you know, colour and ritual and ceremony and incense and all that jazz. When you're used to that type of thing the other stuff's bound to come a bit drab, see what I mean?"

"Yes, I do," Alec said. "But you've got to remember that's the way we run things." He paused to pick up four of the half-dozen pieces of silver that remained of his two pound notes. "We like our religion to be austere, as you call it."

"Like I said, it's what you're used to."

Alec's voice rose. "And we don't like a lot of dressing-up and chanting and bowing and scraping and any tomfoolery of that kind. That's not what we want in this country. We'll do things the British way . . ."

"Who's we, Uncle Mac? Okay, Ann."

"... which means we're not going to take very kindly, necessarily anyway, to any religion that's . . . and a lot of other things for that matter, that aren't——"

"That are foreign, that what you mean?"

"Yes, if you want to put it like that."

"Well, you want to put it like that, anyway, don't you? It's all right, Ann, honest. Yeah, the Pope does live in Rome, no getting away from that. There's no end of foreign things in this country when you get down to it, like the wine we just drunk, and that cigar you're smoking. And lots of foreign people, too, one sort and another. In fact I remember in my far-distant youth they were always going on at us about that—you know, how anyone could come here and carry on pretty well any way he liked, provided he behaved himself. They used to reckon it was one of the big——"

"It's no use telling old Mac any of that," Bob put in, swivelling his glance round the table: "he thinks the English are foreigners really, don't you, old chap? and the Welsh and the Irish too, of course, and the Highland Scotch, and he's not too happy about Edinburgh and Glasgow; in fact, unless you come from Peebles you're a black man as near as dammit, what?"

Everybody laughed loudly, including Elizabeth and Sonia. Alec joined in with the rest. He would not have wanted to withdraw anything he had said to Frank. There was far too much of this sentimentality about nowadays, the idea that you had to be twice as nice to Negroes and Jews and Indians and so on whatever they were like, which the better types among them must surely resent. And he felt that a little opposition from time to time would not do

Frank any harm. All the same, Alec realised, he had gone rather far. No need to have got hot under the collar like that—it must have looked...Suddenly overheated, he rubbed his hand across his forehead. He had drunk too much whisky on an empty stomach, and he ought to have remembered that white wine never agreed with him. The notion of a few minutes in the open air abruptly became irresistible.

At the side of the building there was a small walled yard, embellished with a few climbing plants, where people could sit and drink in the summer if they cared to fetch their own orders from the saloon bar. The chairs and tables had been removed, no doubt to protect against his own folly anyone whom the sunshine might have lured into the treacherous autumnal outdoors. Alec perched himself on a low brick wall and was clasping his hands round one knee, pipe in mouth, when he was joined by Annette, who must have followed him more or less straight from the dining-room. She remained standing, a rather dumpy figure without trace of her mother's looks.

He took her expression for one of inquiry. "I'm all right," he said. "It was a bit stuffy in there, wasn't it?"

"I didn't like what you said to Frank just now."

"I know, I'm sorry, Annette, I didn't think."

"You knew he was in the Army for six years and got captured in North Africa? That makes him as British as anyone else as far as I'm concerned. That and having a naturalised British father and a mother born British and being born in England himself. And who cares anyway? And do you know how many Catholics there are in England? And it was all Catholics here once, before they——"

"Annette, I really am sorry. I had no intention of——"

"He's the best husband and father anyone could wish for. Never looks at another woman even though I know he gets plenty of chances. And then he runs into this kind of muck. He gets it in business all the time. 'Mister who? How do you spell that? Oh.' You can tell what they're thinking, that's when they don't come out and say it. I get it too, you see. 'How long's your husband been over here?' It makes me mad. She was always going on about it. Fine Liberal she was."

"But she wouldn't ever have dreamt of——"

"You didn't know her. The way she used to go on about Elizabeth. That's a laugh, isn't it, 'Elizabeth'? That was him—you don't think I'd have been the one who wanted to name——"

The sunlight suddenly grew more intense and Alec shaded his eyes with the hand that held the pipe. "What? I don't quite——"

"Never mind. She's well developed for her age, I know, but these days a lot of them are, with the diet or whatever it is. She'd never let me alone about it—I'd see her watching the kid, sort of fascinated, and then when we were by ourselves she'd say, 'She's so *big*, isn't she?' as if it was... nasty or disgusting or something. 'She's so *big*,' she'd say, as if I'd done it on purpose to spite her. And then she'd say, 'Of course, these Italian girls, they're women at fourteen, aren't they? Like Jewesses.' Her own granddaughter. Three-quarters English. I don't think she ever believed Frank isn't a Jew really and hadn't taken up being a Catholic as a sort of extra. She never liked him and she didn't mind showing it, either."

"But Annette, it was your father who was against Frank

if either of them was; I remember them arguing about it. He said——"

"You know what Dad's like, up in the air one minute and forgotten all about it the next, it's just his way. No, she was the one. It wasn't like her to come out and say anything; all smiles on the surface and needling away whenever she got the chance. She was the same with Sonia's eyesight and Chris crying too much according to her. I often say to myself the only grandchildren she'd really like would be if Charlie and I got together and had some. She gave him a hell of a time, I don't know whether you knew, wanting to know where he was and who he was with all the time. He got away overseas as soon as he could, poor old Charlie."

Annette stopped, not looking at Alec, who hugged his knees tighter to prevent them from trembling. "I didn't realise you hated her," he said.

"I didn't hate her, Uncle Mac—been easier if I had, in a way. Oh, she was all right in lots of ways and she did enjoy a laugh. It was the way she wouldn't ever leave me and my marriage and my kids alone made me mad." At the mention of anger, anger itself returned to her voice, which had softened in the last minute or so. "She liked baby-sitting when she came to stay because that gave her a chance to snoop around. She kept you on a pretty good string, didn't she, too, all these years? I felt sorry for you. Dad told me about it once when they'd had one of their rows. He didn't really mind because it gave her a bit of a kick. Mind you, according to him she let it slip once she thought early on you were going to ask her to go off with you, but then you never did. Why not?"

"It wasn't that sort of love," Alec said.

"No, I know the sort. That's the best sort, the sort you
don't have to do anything about or get to know the person,
and it was fine for her. The way she used to put on a big
tolerant act Sunday mornings when we came back from
Mass when we stayed with them. Tolerant."

Alec thought he saw tears of rage and grief in her eyes.
He got up and put his arm diffidently round her shoulders.
She went on standing in the same position with her weight
on both feet, not stiffening or drawing away, but not relaxing against him either. What she had said had affected him
chiefly with apprehension that she might lose all self-control.
Whether or not her view of her mother was true, or truer
than his, he still felt as if he had spent thirty-two years preparing a gift that had had, and could conceivably have had,
no recipient. In return for his trouble he retained, safe
against total erosion, Betty's gift to him of a few ideas about
what human nature was like; and the last two or three
hours had taught him something of how envy and pride
could appreciably distort his judgment of other people. All
this amounted to more than a little, without being, of
course, anywhere near enough. He dropped his arm to his side.

Annette said: "We'd better be getting back in. I'm sorry
I came out with some of that. I didn't want to hurt your
feelings—it was just that——"

"We've all been under a great strain."

"You come back with us, Uncle Mac, and have some
supper, there's plenty of stuff in. Frank'll run you home."

"That's very kind of you, but it's right across London,
you know."

"Doesn't matter. We ought to see more of you. Seems
silly not to."

"It's a pity it's such a long way."

SOMETHING STRANGE

SOMETHING STRANGE

SOMETHING STRANGE HAPPENED every day. It might happen during the morning, while the two men were taking their readings and observations and the two women busy with the domestic routine: the big faces had come during the morning. Or, as with the little faces and the coloured fires, the strange thing would happen in the afternoon, in the middle of Bruno's maintenance programme and Clovis's transmission to Base, Lia's rounds of the garden and Myri's work on her story. The evening was often undisturbed, the night less often.

They all understood that ordinary temporal expressions had no meaning for people confined indefinitely, as they were, to a motionless steel sphere hanging in a region of space so empty that the light of the nearest star took some hundreds of years to reach them. The Standing Orders devised by Base, however, recommended that they adopt a twenty-four-hour unit of time, as was the rule on the Earth they had not seen for many months. The arrangement suited them well: their work, recreation and rest seemed to fall naturally into the periods provided. It was only the prospect of year after year of the same routine, stretching farther into the future than they could see, that was a source of strain.

Bruno commented on this to Clovis after a morning spent repairing a fault in the spectrum analyser they used for investigating and classifying the nearer stars. They were sitting at the main observation port in the lounge, drinking the midday cocktail and waiting for the women to join them.

"I'd say we stood up to it extremely well," Clovis said in answer to Bruno. "Perhaps too well."

Bruno hunched his fat figure upright. "How do you mean?"

"We may be hindering our chances of being relieved."

"Base has never said a word about our relief."

"Exactly. With half a million stations to staff, it'll be a long time before they get round to one like this, where everything runs smoothly. You and I are a perfect team, and you have Lia and I have Myri, and they're all right together—no real conflict at all. Hence no reason for a relief."

Myri had heard all this as she laid the table in the alcove. She wondered how Clovis could not know that Bruno wanted to have her instead of Lia, or perhaps as well as Lia. If Clovis did know, and was teasing Bruno, then that would be a silly thing to do, because Bruno was not a pleasant man. With his thick neck and pale fat face he would not be pleasant to be had by, either, quite unlike Clovis, who was no taller but whose straight, hard body and soft skin were always pleasant. He could not think as well as Bruno, but on the other hand many of the things Bruno thought were not pleasant. She poured herself a drink and went over to them.

Bruno had said something about its being a pity they could not fake their personnel report by inventing a few quarrels, and Clovis had immediately agreed that that was impossible. She kissed him and sat down at his side. "What do you think about the idea of being relieved?" he asked her.

"I never think about it."

"Quite right," Bruno said, grinning. "You're doing very nicely here. Fairly nicely, anyway."

"What are you getting at?" Clovis asked him with a different kind of grin.

"It's not a very complete life, is it? For any of us. I could do with a change, anyway. A different kind of job, something that isn't testing and using and repairing apparatus. We do seem to have a lot of repairing to do, don't we? That analyser breaks down almost every day. And yet——"

His voice tailed off and he looked out of the port, as if to assure himself that all that lay beyond it was the familiar starscape of points and smudges of light.

"And yet what?" Clovis asked, irritably this time.

"I was just thinking that we really ought to be thankful for having plenty to do. There's the routine, and the fruits and vegetables to look after, and Myri's story.... How's that going, by the way? Won't you read us some of it? This evening, perhaps?"

"Not until it's finished, if you don't mind."

"Oh, but I do mind. It's part of our duty to entertain one another. And I'm very interested in it personally."

"Why?"

"Because you're an interesting girl. Bright brown eyes and a healthy glowing skin—how do you manage it after all this time in space? And you've more energy than any of us."

Myri said nothing. Bruno was good at making remarks there was nothing to say to.

"What's it about, this story of yours?" he pursued. "At least you can tell us that."

"I have told you. It's about normal life. Life on Earth before there were any space stations, lots of different people doing different things, not this——"

"That's normal life, is it, different people doing different things? I can't wait to hear what the things are. Who's the hero, Myri? Our dear Clovis?"

Myri put her hand on Clovis's shoulder. "No more, please, Bruno. Let's go back to your point about the routine. I couldn't understand why you left out the most important part, the part that keeps us busiest of all."

"Ah, the strange happenings." Bruno dipped his head in a characteristic gesture, half laugh, half nervous tremor. "And the hours we spend discussing them. Oh yes. How could I have failed to mention all that?"

"If you've got any sense you'll go on not mentioning it," Clovis snapped. "We're all fed up with the whole business."

"You may be, but I'm not. I want to discuss it. So does Myri, don't you, Myri?"

"I do think perhaps it's time we made another attempt to find a pattern," Myri said. This was a case of Bruno not being pleasant but being right.

"Oh, not again." Clovis bounded up and went over to the drinks table. "Ah, hallo, Lia," he said to the tall, thin, blonde woman who had just entered with a tray of cold dishes. "Let me get you a drink. Bruno and Myri are getting philosophical—looking for patterns. What do you think? I'll tell you what I think. I think we're doing enough already. I think patterns are Base's job."

"We can make it ours, too," Bruno said. "You agree, Lia?"

"Of course," Lia said in the deep voice that seemed to Myri to carry so much more firmness and individuality in its tone than any of its owner's words or actions.

"Very well. You can stay out of this if you like, Clovis. We start from the fact that what we see and hear need not be illusions, although they may be."

"At least that they're illusions that any human being might have, they're not special to us, as we know from Base's reports of what happens to other stations."

"Correct, Myri. In any event, illusions or not, they are being directed at us by an intelligence and for a purpose."

"We don't know that," Myri objected. "They may be natural phenomena, or the by-product of some intelligent activity not directed at us."

"Correct again, but let us reserve these less probable possibilities until later. Now, as a sample, consider the last week's strange happenings. I'll fetch the log so that there can be no dispute."

"I wish you'd stop it," Clovis said when Bruno had gone out to the apparatus room. "It's a waste of time."

"Time's the only thing we're not short of."

"I'm not short of anything," he said, touching her thigh. "Come with me for a little while."

"Later."

"Lia always goes with Bruno when he asks her."

"Oh yes, but that's my choice," Lia said. "She doesn't want to now. Wait until she wants to."

"I don't like waiting."

"Waiting can make it better."

"Here we are," Bruno said briskly, returning. "Right.... Monday. *Within a few seconds the sphere became encased in a thick brownish damp substance that tests revealed to be both impermeable and infinitely thick. No action by the staff suggested itself. After three hours and eleven minutes the substance disappeared.* It's the *infinitely thick* thing that's interesting. That must have been an illusion, or something would have happened to all the other stations at the same time, not to speak of the stars and planets. A total or partial illusion, then. Agreed?"

"Go on."

"Tuesday. *Metallic object of size comparable to that of the sphere approaching on collision course at 500 kilometres per second. No countermeasures available. Object appeared instantaneously at 35 million kilometres' distance and disappeared instantaneously at 1500 kilometres.* What about that?"

"We've had ones like that before," Lia put in. "Only this was the longest time it's taken to approach and the nearest it's come before disappearing."

"Incomprehensible or illusion," Myri suggested.

"Yes, I think that's the best we can do at the moment. Wednesday: a very trivial one, not worth discussing. *A being apparently constructed entirely of bone approached the main port and made beckoning motions.* Whoever's doing this must be running out of ideas. Thursday. *All bodies external to the sphere vanished to all instruments simultaneously, reappearing to all instruments simultaneously two hours later.* That's not a new one either, I seem to remember. Illusion? Good. Friday. *Beings resembling terrestrial reptiles covered the sphere, fighting ceaselessly and eating portions of one another. Loud rustling and slithering sounds.* The sounds at least must have been an illusion, with no air out there, and I never heard of a reptile that didn't breathe. The same sort of thing applies to yesterday's performance. *Human screams of pain and extreme astonishment approaching and receding. No visual or other accompaniment.*" He paused and looked round at them. "Well? Any uniformities suggest themselves?"

"No," Clovis said, helping himself to salad, for they sat now at the lunch table. "And I defy any human brain to devise any. The whole thing's arbitrary."

"On the contrary, the very next happening—today's when it comes—might reveal an unmistakable pattern."

"The one to concentrate on," Myri said, "is the approaching object. Why did it vanish before striking the sphere?"

Bruno stared at her. "It had to, if it was an illusion."

"Not at all. Why couldn't we have had an illusion of the sphere being struck? And supposing it wasn't an illusion?"

"Next time there's an object, perhaps it will strike," Lia said.

Clovis laughed. "That's a good one. What would happen if it did, I wonder? And it wasn't an illusion?"

They all looked at Bruno for an answer. After a moment or two, he said: "I presume the sphere would shatter and we'd all be thrown into space. I simply can't imagine what that would be like. We should be...Never to see one another again, or anybody or anything else, to be nothing more than a senseless lump floating in space for ever. The chances of——"

"It would be worth something to be rid of your conversation," Clovis said, amiable again now that Bruno was discomfited. "Let's be practical for a change. How long will it take you to run off your analyses this afternoon? There's a lot of stuff to go out to Base and I shan't be able to give you a hand."

"An hour, perhaps, after I've run the final tests."

"Why run tests at all? She was lined up perfectly when we finished this morning."

"Fortunately."

"Fortunately indeed. One more variable and we might have found it impossible."

"Yes," Bruno said abstractedly. Then he got to his feet so abruptly that the other three started. "But we didn't, did we? There wasn't one more variable, was there? It didn't quite happen, you see, the thing we couldn't handle."

Nobody spoke.

"Excuse me, I must be by myself."

"If Bruno keeps this up," Clovis said to the two women, "Base will send up a relief sooner than we think."

Myri tried to drive the thought of Bruno's strange behaviour out of her head when, half an hour later, she sat down to work on her story. The expression on his face as he left the table had been one she could not name. Excitement? Dislike? Surprise? That was the nearest—a kind of persistent surprise. Well, he was certain, being Bruno, to set about explaining it at dinner. She wished he were more pleasant, because he did think well.

Finally expelling the image of Bruno's face, she began

rereading the page of manuscript she had been working on when the screams had interrupted her the previous afternoon. It was part of a difficult scene, one in which a woman met by chance a man who had been having her ten years earlier, with the complication that she was at the time in the company of the man who was currently having her. The scene was an eating alcove in a large city.

"Go away," Volsci said, "or I'll hit you."

Norbu smiled in a not-pleasant way. "What good would that do? Irmy likes me better than she likes you. You are more pleasant, no doubt, but she likes me better. She remembers me having her ten years ago more clearly than she remembers you having her last night. I am good at thinking, which is better than any amount of being pleasant."

"She's having her meal with me," Volsci said, pointing to the cold food and drinks in front of them. "Aren't you, Irmy?"

"Yes, Irmy," Norbu said. "You must choose. If you can't let both of us have you, you must say which of us you like better."

Irmy looked from one man to the other. There was so much difference between them that she could hardly begin to choose: The one more pleasant, the other better at thinking, the one slim, the other plump. She decided being pleasant was better. It was more important and more significant—better in every way that made a real difference. She said: "I'll have Volsci."

Norbu looked surprised and sorry. "I think you're wrong."

"You might as well go now," Volsci said. "Ila will be waiting."

"Yes," Norbu said. He looked extremely sorry now.

Irmy felt quite sorry too. "Goodbye, Norbu," she said.

Myri smiled to herself. It was good, even better than she had remembered—there was no point in being modest inside one's own mind. She must be a real writer in spite of Bruno's scoffing, or how could she have invented these characters, who were so utterly unlike anybody she knew, and then put them into a situation that was so completely outside her experience? The only thing she was not sure about was whether she might not have overplayed the part about feeling or dwelt on it at too great length. Perhaps *extremely sorry* was a little heavy; she replaced it by *sorrier than before*. Excellent: now there was just the right touch of restraint in the middle of all the feeling. She decided she could finish off the scene in a few lines.

"Probably see you at some cocktail hour," Volsci said, she wrote, then looked up with a frown as the buzzer sounded at her door. She crossed her tiny wedge-shaped room—its rear wall was part of the outer wall of the sphere, but it had no port—threw the lock and found Bruno on the threshold. He was breathing fast, as if he had been hurrying or lifting a heavy weight, and she saw with distaste that there were drops of sweat on his thick skin. He pushed past her and sat down on her bed, his mouth open.

"What is it?" she asked, displeased. The afternoon was a private time unless some other arrangement were made at lunch.

"I don't know what it is. I think I must be ill."

"Ill? But you can't be. Only people on Earth get ill. Nobody on a station is ever ill: Base told us that. Illness is caused by——"

"I don't think I believe some of the things that Base says."

"But who can we believe if we don't believe Base?"

Bruno evidently did not hear her question. He said: "I had to come to you—Lia's no good for this. Please let me stay with you, I've got so much to say."

"It's no use, Bruno. Clovis is the one who has me. I thought you understood that I didn't——"

"That's not what I mean," he said impatiently. "Where I need you is in thinking. Though that's connected with the other, the having. I don't expect you to see that. I've only just begun to see it myself."

Myri could make nothing of this last part. "Thinking? Thinking about what?"

He bit his lip and shut his eyes for a moment. "Listen to this," he said. "It was the analyser that set my mind going. Almost every other day it breaks down. And the computer, the counters, the repellers, the scanners and the rest of them —they're always breaking down too, and so are their power supplies. But not the purifier or the fluid-reconstitutor or the fruit and vegetable growers or the heaters or the main power source. Why not?"

"Well, they're less complicated. How can a fruit grower go wrong? A chemical tank and a water tank is all there is to it. You ask Lia about that."

"All right. Try answering this, then. The strange happenings. If they're illusions, why are they always outside the sphere? Why are there never any inside?"

"Perhaps there are," Myri said.

"Don't. I don't want that. I shouldn't like that. I want everything in here to be real. Are you real? I must believe you are."

"Of course I'm real." She was now thoroughly puzzled.

"And it makes a difference, doesn't it? It's very important that you and everything else should be real, everything in the sphere. But tell me : whatever's arranging these happenings must be pretty powerful if it can fool our instruments and our senses so completely and consistently, and yet it can't do anything—anything we recognise as strange, that is—inside this puny little steel skin. Why not?"

"Presumably it has its limitations. We should be pleased."

"Yes. All right, next point. You remember the time I tried to sit up in the lounge after midnight and stay awake?"

"That was silly. Nobody can stay awake after midnight. Standing Orders were quite clear on that point."

"Yes, they were, weren't they?" Bruno seemed to be trying to grin. "Do you remember my telling you how I couldn't account for being in my own bed as usual when the music woke us—you remember the big music? And—this is what I'm really after—do you remember how we all agreed at breakfast that life in space must have conditioned us in such a way that falling asleep at a fixed time had become an automatic mechanism? You remember that?"

"Naturally I do."

"Right. Two questions, then. Does that strike you as a likely explanation? That sort of complete self-conditioning in all four of us after ... just a number of months?"

"Not when you put it like that."

"But we all agreed on it, didn't we? Without hesitation."

Myri, leaning against a side wall, fidgeted. He was being not pleasant in a new way, one that made her want to stop him talking even while he was thinking at his best. "What's your other question, Bruno?" Her voice sounded unusual to her.

"Ah, you're feeling it too, are you?"

"I don't know what you mean."

"I think you will in a minute. Try my other question. The night of the music was a long time ago, soon after we arrived here, but you remember it clearly. So do I. And yet when I try to remember what I was doing only a couple of months earlier, on Earth, finishing up my life there, getting ready for this, it's just a vague blur. Nothing stands out."

"It's all so remote."

"Maybe. But I remember the trip clearly enough, don't you?"

Myri caught her breath. I feel surprised, she told herself. Or something like that. I feel the way Bruno looked when he left the lunch table. She said nothing.

"You're feeling it now all right, aren't you?" He was watching her closely with his narrow eyes. "Let me try to describe it. A surprise that goes on and on. Puzzlement. Symptoms of physical exertion or strain. And above all a . . . a sort of discomfort, only in the mind. Like having a sharp object pressed against a tender part of your body, except that this is in your mind."

"What are you talking about?"

"A difficulty of vocabulary."

The loudspeaker above the door clicked on and Clovis's voice said: "Attention. Strange happening. Assemble in the lounge at once. Strange happening."

Myri and Bruno stopped staring at each other and hurried out along the narrow corridor. Clovis and Lia were already in the lounge, looking out of the port.

Apparently only a few feet beyond the steelhard glass, and illuminated from some invisible source, were two floating. figures. The detail was excellent, and the four inside the sphere could distinguish without difficulty every fold in the naked skin of the two caricatures of humanity presented, it seemed, for their thorough inspection, a presumption given added weight by the slow rotation of the pair that enabled their every portion to be scrutinised. Except for a scrubby growth at the base of the skull, they were hairless. The limbs were foreshortened, lacking the normal narrowing at the joints, and the bellies protuberant. One had male characteristics, the other female, yet in neither case were these complete. From each open, wet, quivering toothless mouth there came a loud, clearly audible yelling, higher in pitch than any those in the sphere could have produced, and of an unfamiliar emotional range.

"Well, I wonder how long this will last," Clovis said.

"Is it worth trying the repellers on them?" Lia asked. "What does the radar say? Does it see them?"

"I'll go and have a look."

Bruno turned his back on the port. "I don't like them."

"Why not?" Myri saw he was sweating again.

"They remind me of something."

"What?"

"I'm trying to think."

But although Bruno went on trying to think for the rest of that day, with such obvious seriousness that even Clovis did his best to help with suggestions, he was no nearer a solution when they parted, as was their habit, at five minutes to midnight. And when, several times in the next

couple of days, Myri mentioned the afternoon of the caricatures to him, he showed little interest.

"Bruno, you are extraordinary," she said one evening.
"What happened to those odd feelings of yours you were so
eager to describe to me just before Clovis called us into the
lounge?"

He shrugged his narrow shoulders in the almost girlish
way he had. "Oh, I don't know what could have got into
me," he said. "I expect I was just angry with the con-
founded analyser and the way it kept breaking down. It's
been much better recently."

"And all that thinking you used to do."

"That was a complete waste of time."

"Surely not."

"Yes, I agree with Clovis, let Base do all the thinking."

Myri was disappointed. To hear Bruno resigning the task
of thought seemed like the end of something. This feeling
was powerfully underlined for her when, a little later, the
announcement came over the loudspeaker in the lounge.
Without any preamble at all, other than the usual click on,
a strange voice said: "Your attention, please. This is Base
calling over your intercom."

They all looked up in great surprise, especially Clovis,
who said quickly to Bruno: "Is that possible?"

"Oh yes, they've been experimenting," Bruno replied
as quickly.

"It is perhaps ironical," the voice went on, "that the first
transmission we have been able to make to you by the
present means is also the last you will receive by any. For
some time the maintenance of space stations has been un-
economic, and the decision has just been taken to dis-
continue them altogether. You will therefore make no

further reports of any kind, or rather you may of course continue to do on the understanding that nobody will be listening. In many cases it has fortunately been found possible to arrange for the collection of station staffs and their return to Earth : in others, those involving a journey to the remoter parts of the galaxy, a prohibitive expenditure of time and effort would be entailed. I am sorry to have to tell you that your own station is one of these. Accordingly, you will never be relieved. All of us here are confident that you will respond to this new situation with dignity and resource.

"Before we sever communication for the last time, I have one more point to make. It involves a revelation which may prove so unwelcome that only with the greatest reluctance can I bring myself to utter it. My colleagues, however, insisted that those in your predicament deserve, in your own interests, to hear the whole truth about it. I must tell you, then, that contrary to your earlier information we have had no reports from any other station whose content resembles in the slightest degree your accounts of the strange happenings you claim to have witnessed. The deception was considered necessary so that your morale might be maintained, but the time for deceptions is over. You are unique, and in the variety of mankind that is no small distinction. Be proud of it. Goodbye for ever."

They sat without speaking until five minutes to midnight. Try as she would, Myri found it impossible to conceive their future, and the next morning she had no more success. That was as long as any of them had leisure to come to terms with their permanent isolation, for by midday a quite new phase of strange happenings had begun. Myri and Lia were preparing lunch in the kitchen when Myri, opening the cupboard where the dishes were kept, was confronted by a flattish, reddish creature with many legs and a pair of unequally sized pincers. She gave a gasp, almost a shriek, of astonishment.

"What is it?" Lia said, hurrying over, and then in a high voice: "Is it alive?"

"It's moving. Call the men."

Until the others came, Myri simply stared. She found her lower lip shaking in a curious way. *Inside* now, she kept thinking. Not just outside. *Inside.*

"Let's have a look," Clovis said. "I see. Pass me a knife or something." He rapped at the creature, making a dry, bony sound. "Well, it works for tactile and aural, as well as visual, anyway. A thorough illusion. If it is one."

"It must be," Bruno said. "Don't you recognise it?"

"There is something familiar about it, I suppose."

"You suppose? You mean you don't know a crab when you see one?"

"Oh, of course," Clovis looked slightly sheepish. "I remember now. A terrestrial animal, isn't it? Lives in the water. And so it must be an illusion. Crabs don't cross space as far as I know, and even if they could they'd have a tough time carving their way through the skin of the sphere."

His sensible manner and tone helped Myri to get over her astonishment, and it was she who suggested that the crab be disposed of down the waste chute. At lunch, she said: "It was a remarkably specific illusion, don't you think? I wonder how it was projected."

"No point in wondering about that," Bruno told her. "How can we ever know? And what use would the knowledge be to us if we did know?"

"Knowing the truth has its own value."

"I don't understand you."

Lia came in with the coffee just then. "The crab's back," she said. "Or there's another one there, I can't tell."

More crabs, or simulacra thereof, appeared at intervals for the rest of the day, eleven of them in all. It seemed, as Clovis put it, that the illusion-producing technique had its limitations, inasmuch as none of them saw a crab actually materialise : the new arrival would be "discovered" under a bed or behind a bank of apparatus. On the other hand, the depth of illusion produced was very great, as they all agreed when Myri, putting the eighth crab down the chute, was nipped in the finger, suffered pain and exuded a few drops of blood.

"Another new departure," Clovis said. "An illusory physical process brought about on the actual person of one of us. They're improving."

Next morning there were the insects. The main apparatus room was found to be infested with what, again on Bruno's prompting, they recognised as cockroaches. By lunch-time there were moths and flying beetles in all the main rooms, and a number of large flies became noticeable towards the evening. The whole of their attention became concentrated upon avoiding these creatures as far as possible. The day passed without Clovis asking Myri to go with him. This had never happened before.

The following afternoon a fresh problem was raised by Lia's announcement that the garden now contained no fruits or vegetables—none, at any rate, that were accessible to her senses. In this the other three concurred. Clovis put the feelings of all of them when he said : "If this is an illusion, it's as efficient as the reality, because fruits and vegetables you can never find are the same as no fruits and vegetables."

The evening meal used up all the food they had. Soon after two o'clock in the morning Myri was aroused by Clovis's voice saying over the loudspeaker: "Attention, everyone. Strange happening. Assemble in the lounge immediately."

She was still on her way when she became aware of a new quality in the background of silence she had grown used to. It was a deeper silence, as if some sound at the very threshold of audibility had ceased. There were unfamiliar vibrations underfoot.

Clovis was standing by the port, gazing through it with interest. "Look at this, Myri," he said.

At a distance impossible to gauge, an oblong of light had become visible, a degree or so in breadth and perhaps two and a half times as high. The light was of comparable quality to that illuminating the inside of the sphere. Now and then it flickered.

"What is it?" Myri asked.

"I don't know, it's only just appeared." The floor beneath them shuddered violently. "That was what woke me, one of those tremors. Ah, here you are, Bruno. What do you make of it?"

Bruno's large eyes widened further, but he said nothing. A moment later Lia arrived and joined the silent group by the port. Another vibration shook the sphere. Some vessel in the kitchen fell to the floor and smashed. Then Myri said: "I can see what looks like a flight of steps leading down from the lower edge of the light. Three or four of them, perhaps more."

She had barely finished speaking when a shadow

appeared before them, cast by the rectangle of light on to a surface none of them could identify. The shadow seemed to them of a stupefying vastness, but it was beyond question that of a man. A moment later the man came into view, outlined by the light, and descended the steps. Another moment or two and he was evidently a few feet from the port, looking in on them, their own lights bright on the upper half of him. He was a well-built man wearing a grey uniform jacket and a metal helmet. An object recognisable as a gun of some sort was slung over his shoulder. While he watched them, two other figures, similarly accoutred, came down the steps and joined him. There was a brief interval, then he moved out of view to their right, doing so with the demeanour of one walking on a level surface.

None of the four inside spoke or moved, not even at the sound of heavy bolts being drawn in the section of outer wall directly in front of them, not even when that entire section swung away from them like a door opening outwards and the three men stepped through into the sphere. Two of them had unslung the guns from their shoulders.

Myri remembered an occasion, weeks ago, when she had risen from a stooping position in the kitchen and struck her head violently on the bottom edge of a cupboard door Lia had happened to leave open. The feeling Myri now experienced was similar, except that she had no particular physical sensations. Another memory, a much fainter one, passed across the far background of her mind: somebody had once tried to explain to her the likeness between a certain mental state and the bodily sensation of discomfort, and she had not understood. The memory faded sharply.

The man they had first seen said: "All roll up your sleeves."

Clovis looked at him with less curiosity than he had been showing when Myri first joined him at the port, a few minutes earlier. "You're an illusion," he said.

"No I'm not. Roll up your sleeves, all of you."

He watched them closely while they obeyed, becoming impatient at the slowness with which they moved. The other man whose gun was unslung, a younger man, said: "Don't be hard on them, Allen. We've no idea what they've been through."

"I'm not taking any chances," Allen said. "Not after that crowd in the trees. Now this is for your own good," he went on, addressing the four. "Keep quite still. All right, Douglas."

The third man came forward, holding what Myri knew to be a hypodermic syringe. He took her firmly by her bare arm and gave her an injection. At once her feelings altered, in the sense that, although there was still discomfort in her mind, neither this nor anything else seemed to matter.

After a time she heard the young man say: "You can roll your sleeves down now. You can be quite sure that nothing bad will happen to you."

"Come with us," Allen said.

Myri and the others followed the three men out of the sphere, across a gritty floor that might have been concrete and up the steps, a distance of perhaps thirty feet. They entered a corridor with artificial lighting and then a room into which the sun was streaming. There were twenty or thirty people in the room, some of them wearing the grey uniform. Now and then the walls shook as the sphere had done, but to the accompaniment of distant explosions. A faint shouting could also be heard from time to time.

Allen's voice said loudly: "Let's try and get a bit of order going. Douglas, they'll be wanting you to deal with the people in the tank. They've been conditioned to believe they're congenitally aquatic, so you'd better give them a shot that'll knock them out straight away. Holmes is draining the tank now. Off you go. Now you, James, you watch this lot while I find out some more about them. I wish those psycho chaps would turn up—we're just working in the dark." His voice moved further away. "Sergeant—get these five out of here."

"Where to, sir?"

"I don't mind where—just out of here. And watch them."

"They've all been given shots, sir."

"I know, but look at them, they're not human any more. And it's no use talking to them, they've been deprived of language. That's how they got the way they are. Now get them out right away."

Myri looked slowly at the young man who stood near them: James. "Where are we?" she asked.

James hesitated. "I was ordered to tell you nothing," he said. "You're supposed to wait for the psychological team to get to you and treat you."

"Please."

"All right. This much can't hurt you, I suppose. You four and a number of other groups have been the subject of various experiments. This building is part of Special Welfare Research Station No. 4. Or rather it was. The government that set it up no longer exists. It has been removed by the revolutionary army of which I'm a member. We had to shoot our way in here and there's fighting still going on."

"Then we weren't in space at all."

"No."

"Why did they make us believe we were?"

"We don't know yet."

"And how did they do it?"

"Some new form of deep-level hypnosis, it seems, probably renewed at regular intervals. Plus various apparatus for producing illusions. We're still working on that. Now, I think that's enough questions for the moment. The best thing you can do is sit down and rest."

"Thank you. What's hypnosis?"

"Oh, of course they'd have removed knowledge of that. It'll all be explained to you later."

"James, come and have a look at this, will you?" Allen's voice called. "I can't make much of it."

Myri followed James a little way. Among the clamour of voices, some speaking languages unfamiliar to her, others speaking none, she heard James ask: "Is this the right file? Fear Elimination?"

"Must be," Allen answered. "Here's the last entry. *Removal of Bruno V and substitution of Bruno VI accomplished, together with memory-adjustment of other three subjects. Memo to Preparation Centre: avoid repetition of Bruno V personality-type with strong curiosity-drives.* Started catching on to the set-up, eh? Wonder what they did with him."

"There's that psycho hospital across the way they're still investigating; perhaps he's in there."

"With Brunos I to IV, no doubt. Never mind that for

the moment. Now. *Procedures: penultimate phase. Removal of all ultimate confidence: severance of communication, total denial of prospective change, inculcation of "uniqueness" syndrome, environment shown to be violable, unknowable crisis in prospect (food deprivation).* I can understand that last bit. They don't look starved, though."

"Perhaps they've only just started them on it."

"We'll get them fed in a minute. Well, all this still beats me, James. *Reactions. Little change. Responses poor. Accelerating impoverishment of emotional life and its vocabulary: compare portion of novel written by Myri VII with contributions of predecessors. Prognosis: further affective deterioration: catatonic apathy: failure of experiment.* That's a comfort, anyway. But what has all this got to do with fear elimination?"

They stopped talking suddenly and Myri followed the direction of their gaze. A door had been opened and the man called Douglas was supervising the entry of a number of others, each supporting or carrying a human form wrapped in a blanket.

"This must be the lot from the tank," Allen or James said.

Myri watched while those in the blankets were made as comfortable as possible on benches or on the floor. One of them, however, remained totally wrapped in his blanket and was paid no attention.

"He's had it, has he?"

"Shock, I'm afraid." Douglas's voice was unsteady. "There was nothing we could do. Perhaps we shouldn't have——"

Myri stooped and turned back the edge of the blanket. What she saw was much stranger than anything she had experienced in the sphere. "What's the matter with him?" she asked James.

"Matter with him? You can die of shock, you know."

"I can do what?"

Myri, staring at James, was aware that his face had become distorted by a mixture of expressions. One of them was understanding: all the others were painful to look at. They were renderings of what she herself was feeling. Her vision darkened and she ran from the room, back the way they had come, down the steps, across the floor, back into the sphere.

James was unfamiliar with the arrangement of the rooms there and did not reach her until she had picked up the manuscript of the novel, hugged it to her chest with crossed arms and fallen on to her bed, her knees drawn up as far as they would go, her head lowered as it had been before her birth, an event of which she knew nothing.

She was still in the same position when, days later, somebody sat heavily down beside her. "Myri. You must know who this is. Open your eyes, Myri. Come out of there."

After he had said this, in the same gentle voice, some hundreds of times, she did open her eyes a little. She was in a long, high room, and near her was a fat man with a pale skin. He reminded her of something to do with space and thinking. She screwed her eyes shut.

"Myri. I know you remember me. Open your eyes again."

She kept them shut while he went on talking.

"Open your eyes. Straighten your body."

She did not move.

"Straighten your body, Myri. I love you."

Slowly her feet crept down the bed and her head lifted.